This book belongs to
Evan Litzkow

JAZZ, PIZZAZZ, and the Silver Threads

JAZZ, PIZZAZZ, and the Silver Threads

Mary Quattlebaum
Illustrated by Robin Oz

Delacorte Press

Published by
Delacorte Press
Bantam Doubleday Dell Publishing Group, Inc.
1540 Broadway
New York, New York 10036

Library of Congress Cataloging-in-Publication Data
Quattlebaum, Mary.
     Jazz, Pizzazz, and the silver threads / Mary Quattlebaum ; illustrated by Robin Oz.
          p.   cm.
     Summary: Nine-year-old Calvin's dream of having a pet of his own is partially fulfilled when his neighbor Jenny gets a hamster named Pizzazz for her magic act.
     ISBN 0-385-32183-X
     [1. Hamsters—Fiction.   2. Pets—Fiction   3. Magicians—Fiction.]
I. Oz, Robin, ill.   II. Title.
PZ7.Q19Jaw   1996
[Fic]—dc20   95–21107
                                                                      CIP
                                                                      AC

The text of this book is set in 13.5-point Electra.
Book design by Kimberly M. Adlerman
Manufactured in the United States of America
March 1996
10   9   8   7   6   5   4   3   2   1

To my parents,
whose home held seven kids and
many, many horses, dogs, cows, cats,
ducks, goats, chickens, quail, and, of
course, hamsters.

Click. Whoosh.

Click. Whoosh.

Click. Whoosh.

That sound was driving Calvin cuckoo.

Click. Whoosh.

Each time Jenny clicked her magic wand against the table and—*whoosh!*—a scarf appeared, Calvin felt his attention click up from his history book and *whoosh* away.

Click. Whoosh.

Calvin plugged his ears with his fingers.

Click. Whoosh.

He read. He read to the bottom of the page. But then he couldn't turn the page without unplugging his ears, and if he unplugged his ears

1

that *click-whoosh* sound would start bugging his brain again.

But if he didn't keep reading, he wouldn't finish his homework. And if he didn't finish his homework, then he couldn't check Ms. Eva's mail before Dad phoned to tell him to come downstairs to his own apartment. The best part of staying at Ms. Eva's apartment after school was checking Ms. Eva's mail. Calvin liked taking the little silver mailbox key and the extra apartment key from the hook in the kitchen. He liked zooming down the elevator to check the neat row of mailboxes in the lobby. He liked looking at the different stamps and reading the return addresses and running his finger along the many envelopes. Calvin liked getting mail, even if it was someone else's.

Ms. Eva let him get the mail each afternoon—*if* he finished his homework.

How could he finish his homework with his fingers plugging his ears?

But, then, how could he finish his homework with that magic-wand *click-whoosh* bugging his brain?

Calvin decided to move quickly. He popped out his fingers and dove for the page.

CLICK. WHOOSH!

"Jenny!" Calvin banged his book shut. "Don't you ever get tired of making those scarves?"

"Nope," said Jenny. She clicked the wand. *Whoosh!* Another scarf bloomed.

Calvin crossed his arms. If checking Ms. Eva's mail was the high point of his afternoon, Jenny's constant magic tricks were a definite low point. Most of the time her tricks were more mess-up than magic. Wands broke. Cards fell. Coins rolled on the floor. But Jenny just kept right on tapping wands, fanning cards, and trying to pull coins from behind someone's ear.

"I think," said Calvin, "your magic is getting on Ms. Eva's nerves."

Jenny glanced at Ms. Eva, who was sitting at her desk and writing. Ms. Eva looked very calm.

"Ms. Eva says my magic is like a *dance*," said Jenny. "Like a dance of scarves."

Calvin did not see how Ms. Eva could possibly say such a thing, but she often did. Personally, he thought Jenny's magic was more like a rattle of cans. Sometimes he wondered why Jenny Teiteltot from Apartment 601 had to stay with Ms. Eva after school. Surely Ms. Eva would be as happy— even happier—with just the Hastings brothers, namely Calvin and his younger brother, Monk, to watch until their parents got home from work.

Ms. Eva never seemed to think so, though.

Jenny cocked her head and regarded Calvin. "I *have* to practice," she said solemnly, "so I can be a great magician. Someday I'll perform before an audience of thousands." She ran the red scarf through her fingers. "Someday I'll be so great that I can turn a scarf—like this ordinary scarf—into an airplane."

Calvin knew he should pretend to be bored. Who cared about Jenny's dumb tricks? Still, he glanced at the red scarf.

He asked. He *had* to ask.

"How can a scarf turn into an airplane?"

Jenny stroked the scarf. "Do you *really* want to know?"

"Yes," said Calvin.

Jenny leaned across the table. "The true magician never reveals her secrets, but"—Jenny lowered her voice—"perhaps I can make *one* exception."

Calvin leaned so far across the table that he teetered on the edge of his chair.

"So you want to know how a scarf can turn into an airplane?" Jenny whispered.

Calvin nodded. His chair tipped forward.

"A scarf can turn into an airplane," Jenny whispered, "by . . ."

4

Calvin's chair tipped farther.

"By *magic!*" Jenny yelled.

"Aargh!" Calvin grabbed for the scarf.

Boom! His chair crashed down.

Jenny peered under the table. "Serves you right," she sniffed at Calvin, who was sprawled on the floor. "A true magician *never* reveals her secrets."

Calvin rose with dignity. Sometimes—and this was one of those times—he couldn't believe that he and Jenny were the same age. Instead of acting nine years old, she behaved like she was two. As he stomped away, Calvin heard *Click!* (Jenny's wand), *Whoosh!* (Jenny's scarf).

"Ms. Eva!" Calvin marched to the desk. "Excuse me," he added.

Ms. Eva looked up from her piece of paper, which was filled with numbers, words, and little dancing stick figures.

"Calvin, dear," she said, "you're slumping."

Calvin sighed and straightened his shoulders. Ms. Eva was a dancer and concerned about graceful posture. When she was young, she had danced with one of the city's best dance companies. Calvin had seen pictures of her leaping gracefully, one knee bent, her bare toes pointed. In these photos, Ms. Eva looked like a wild bird skimming

the air. Now with her friends Roscoe and Alma Rae, Ms. Eva taught jazz dance classes at the YWCA—but she still did everything gracefully. Calvin watched as she smoothed back her gray-streaked hair and gracefully lowered her pencil.

"Ms. Eva," he blurted. "I can't study at the table. Jenny's magic is too noisy."

"Too noisy!" said Ms. Eva. "To me, scarves seem very quiet."

"Not these scarves," said Calvin.

"Why don't you study next to Monk?"

Calvin groaned. If there could be anyone noisier than a clicking, whooshing would-be girl magician it was his brother, Monk. Monk loved to read. In fact, he'd been reading since the age of three, for exactly four years. And each year the books he read grew thicker. The book in Monk's hands now was at least three inches thick! For most people, reading was a quiet activity. Not for Monk. He liked the sound of words. He liked to mumble them as he read. Sometimes he liked to say them right out loud! And the books Monk read were boring, boring, boring. Poetry and stuff like that. And *not* nursery rhymes. No hickory-dickory-dock. No Humpty-Dumpty-sat-on-a-wall. Calvin wasn't sure that some of the words in Monk's books even meant anything. Once Monk had wandered around for three days murmuring "gong-tormented sea." "What does that *mean*?" Calvin had finally yelled. "I don't know," Monk had replied. "But it sure sounds good."

Monk was a kook.

"Ms. Eva," Calvin explained, "I can't study next to Monk. He *reads*."

"Well, you're reading, too," Ms. Eva pointed out.

"I read to myself," said Calvin. "Monk reads to the world. Or to the nearest person. And I don't want that person to be me."

"You can sit in Snuggles and read," said Ms. Eva.

Calvin hated Snuggles. Snuggles was the name of Ms. Eva's special chair. It was designed to *make* you sit gracefully. It was as hard as concrete.

"Snuggles," said Calvin, "is not very comfortable."

"Calvin," Ms. Eva sighed, "you get distracted too easily. You need to learn how to focus."

"Focus," said Calvin.

"Yes," said Ms. Eva. "If you were more focused, you could study anywhere, anytime. Why, if a parade marched by, you wouldn't even hear."

"A parade," said Calvin, "with drums and horns and whistles?"

"Yes," said Ms. Eva.

"I think," said Calvin, "I could still hear a parade with drums and horns and whistles. No one can focus that hard."

"Try," said Ms. Eva.

Calvin slumped into Snuggles. The hard back made him sit as straight as a robot. He opened his book.

Calvin tried to focus. He really tried. He wrinkled his nose. He squinted.

The words on the page jumped and crouched and hopped.

They jumped like puppies and crouched like kittens and hopped about like rabbits.

Not for the first time Calvin wished he had a puppy or a kitten or a rabbit. Something lively to pat, something friendly to hold, a warm buddy in animal skin.

Sometimes Calvin felt lonely after school. Ms. Eva was busy with her dance ideas, Jenny with her scarves, Monk with his mumbled words. Busy, busy, busy.

A pet would be busy, too, Calvin knew. A pet would want to play or be scratched or eat snacks from a bowl. But a pet would be busy with *him*.

And Calvin wanted that kind of busyness, too. Sometimes on Saturdays he would visit Dr.

Jamar's veterinarian's office, which was three blocks from his apartment building. He would sit in the clean waiting room, in a plastic chair, close to a sick puppy or kitten or rabbit. He would pretend that the animal belonged to him and would speak softly to calm its fears. "Don't worry," he would murmur. "You'll feel better soon." In the veterinarian's waiting room on these Saturdays, Calvin could feel the good feeling of having a pet. He felt busy and *very* responsible.

Unfortunately, his parents had picked up the idea that he was *not* responsible. Just because he didn't always finish his homework or clean his side of the room he shared with Monk. Just because he sometimes forgot to bring the trash to the Dumpster.

Calvin even hated the sound of that word "responsible." Re-e-e-e. *Spon*sible. It sounded like a door creaking, then banging shut.

And just last night he had heard it again.

"Calvin," Mom had said, "I don't think you could care for a pet. I just had to remind you about your homework. What if you forgot to feed your dog?"

"He would bark," said Calvin, "to remind me."

"Like I bark about your homework?" said Mom.

"Exactly," said Calvin. "How could I forget?"

10

Mom sighed. "And who would take care of your pet during the day? Dad and I both work. You go to school. Don't you think your pet would get lonely in the city in this small apartment?"

"Mr. Calhoun works," said Calvin, "and he has a cat. I've never seen Lump look lonely."

"I've never seen Lump look anything but mean —and hungry," said Dad.

Dad had a point. Lump, Mr. Calhoun's orange cat, was as big as a dog and hissed like a snake. Lump and Mr. Calhoun lived down the hall from Ms. Eva. Sometimes as he walked to Ms. Eva's, which was Apartment 419, Calvin could hear Lump's fierce pit-viper hiss from behind the door of 415.

"Hey!" Calvin had a brilliant idea. "During the day, my pet could visit Ms. Eva. She probably gets lonely, too."

Mom said, "I think Ms. Eva has enough visitors with you three rapscallions after school."

"Don't you mean scalawags?" Dad asked, smiling from behind his newspaper.

"Or maybe 'rug-runners' would be a better word," Mom mused.

"Excuse me," Calvin interrupted with dignity, "but we were talking about my pet." Honestly, sometimes Mom and Dad were as kooky as Monk.

"Son," said Dad. He made a big show of rattling his paper.

Calvin braced himself. When Dad opened a sentence with "Son," a stream of advice usually followed.

This time was no different.

"Son," Dad said again. (Calvin sighed.) "A pet is a big responsibility. You've got to prove you're ready for that responsibility by behaving in a more responsible manner."

Calvin couldn't believe "responsible" could get wedged three times into one speech.

"Focus a little harder on your schoolwork," said Mom kindly. "Be a little more responsible about your chores at home. Maybe soon we'll get you a nice goldfish."

A *fish!* Calvin thought. How could he pat a fish or hold a fish? A fish might be a *cold* but never a *warm* buddy.

"Dad," said Calvin. "A pet is not the same as homework or chores or trash. I would *want* to be responsible."

"Hmmm," said Dad, returning to his paper.

Sitting in Snuggles, in Ms. Eva's apartment, Calvin repeated to himself, "I would *want* to be responsible." How could he prove he could be responsible for a pet if there was no pet to be responsible for?

Calvin squinted. The words in his book still jumped and crouched and hopped, like puppies and kittens and rabbits. He was still reading the first sentence.

"Calvin," Ms. Eva called. "Calvin! Your father just called from your apartment. It's time to go home."

Calvin stretched. Snuggles had given him a pain in the neck.

"You didn't even hear me," said Ms. Eva. "You must have been focusing *very* hard."

Calvin looked at Ms. Eva.

Ms. Eva looked at him.

"I guess you could say that," said Calvin. "Focusing."

Ms. Eva grinned. She even had a graceful grin. She grinned like she knew Calvin's eyes hadn't moved one inch from the first page, the first paragraph, the first sentence of his book.

"Maybe you can check the mail tomorrow," she said, waving good-bye. "And Calvin, you'll be happy to know there's a chance of snow tonight."

But Calvin didn't hear. He was too busy focusing on getting a real puppy or kitten or rabbit and *not* getting a fish.

As *the city bus rumbled through slush, Calvin* peered out the window and thought about snow.

Calvin loved snow. He loved the fat, flakey look of it falling from the sky. He loved the crisp glitter of it on buildings and cars. He loved the way it draped Dr. Jamar's VETERINARIAN sign, decorated the dingy sidewalks, and flew from Mr. Calhoun's big shovel in front of the art gallery.

Best of all, Calvin loved what snow did to school.

Snow canceled school.

Like today. "All area schools are closed," the radio had announced that morning. On these days, Calvin, Monk, and Jenny stayed with

Ms. Eva until their parents came home from work.

But snow days at Ms. Eva's were very different from after-school days. There was no talk of homework or focusing. Instead, they could play outside, drink hot cocoa, or visit Ms. Eva's dance friends Roscoe and Alma Rae, who lived close to the YWCA. On snow days, it was definitely better to be a kid. The places where grown-ups worked never seemed to close.

As Calvin sat on the city bus, he felt full to bursting with his love of snow.

In the next seat, Ms. Eva considered the dancing stick figures on her piece of paper. In front of Calvin, Monk read his thick book. Jenny wobbled a pencil across her notepad.

Everyone was focused.

Calvin decided to focus. He focused on snow. Snow, snow, snow—what a wonderful sight! Then he focused on Jenny. He knew Jenny had received some money for Christmas and was planning to spend it today. She had told him that she might buy a pet to be part of her magic act. Calvin decided to focus on helping Jenny to find just the right pet. One that would transform her act from mess-up to magic.

Calvin peered over Jenny's shoulder. He read:

scarf (blue)
ball in cup
plastic egg

Calvin knew one thing was missing from that list. A rabbit! Every magician owned a rabbit.

And if Jenny, the would-be girl magician, bought a rabbit, then he, Calvin, could visit the rabbit, help feed the rabbit, maybe hold the rabbit and rub its long ears.

He waited for Jenny to add "rabbit" to her list.

Jenny wrote "scarf (yellow)."

She bit the end of her pencil.

Then she erased "scarf (yellow)."

"Jenny," Calvin pointed out helpfully, "what you need is a rabbit. Every magician has a rabbit."

"Can't have a rabbit," Jenny replied. "Remember my mother's rule?" Jenny recited the rule as if she'd heard it a billion times before. "No dogs, no cats," she said in a singsong, rule-repeating voice, "no ferrets, no parrots, no mice. Nothing larger than a doorknob. The city is no place for a pet any bigger than that." She sighed and said in her normal voice, "I don't think there's any good magic animal smaller than a doorknob."

16

Calvin pictured a rabbit in his mind. He pictured a doorknob. The rabbit, unfortunately, was larger. Much larger.

Calvin imagined other good pets: a cat, a dog, a pony. He placed them beside the doorknob in his mind. Some animals were larger than others. All were larger than the doorknob.

Except for one.

"What about a frog?" Calvin asked.

"Frogs," said Jenny, "have no . . . pizzazz."

"No pizzazz," Calvin repeated.

"They have no energy, no drama," said Jenny. She swept her hand in the air. "They have *zero* pizzazz. All they do is hop."

"Of course they hop," said Calvin. "They're *frogs.*"

"A frog," Jenny sniffed, "is not good magic."

Calvin gave up. Jenny was too picky. At least her mother hadn't told her to be more re-*spon*-sible before she got a pet. All Jenny had to do was focus on size and buy something smaller than a doorknob.

Calvin wished he could trade his parents' rule for Jenny's mother's rule. He would buy a frog so fast that it would make Jenny's scarves spin. Who cared about pizzazz?

The bus rumbled to a stop.

17

Calvin stood up. Jenny stood up.

Monk kept on reading.

"Monk!" said Ms. Eva.

The bus door opened. People tromped off.

"Monk!" hollered Ms. Eva, Calvin, and Jenny.

Monk looked up from his book. He blinked. He smiled.

The door started to swing shut.

Calvin grabbed Monk's sleeve and hauled him off the bus.

"You made me lose my place," grumbled Monk.

"Monk," Calvin sighed, "you sure are focused."

Jenny had already slid ahead on the icy sidewalk and was opening the door to Buster's Magic Shop.

When Calvin entered, he saw Jenny chatting with a fat, bald man. Calvin knew the man was Buster from the trillions of times Jenny had dragged them to the magic shop.

Buster waved a scarf. Jenny watched. Buster gave a dramatic flourish. His moon-face gleamed. Presto!—a key appeared.

Jenny and Buster solemnly examined the scarf.

Calvin peeked over Jenny's shoulder. He wanted to examine the scarf, too.

Jenny and Buster glared at him. "This is *secret*," Jenny said.

Calvin shrugged. Who wanted to look at that

silly scarf anyway? Who cared that it could make a key appear? Jenny would mess up that trick anyway.

Calvin wandered over to a rack lined with items. He saw:

Loaded dice
Vanishing ink
Hand buzzers

"Hey, Jenny!" Calvin tossed an item across the room. "Why don't you make *this* disappear?"

Jenny caught it, glanced at it, dropped it on the counter.

"Honestly, Calvin," she said, wiping her hands on her jeans. "That stuff isn't magic, it's just dumb tricks."

"What's the difference?" Calvin asked. "It sure fooled you!"

They both looked at the plastic dog doo piled on Buster's counter. The brown color was especially realistic, as was the small plastic fly perched on top.

"If you were a real magician"—Jenny tossed back her hair—"you'd know the difference."

" 'If you were a real magician,' " Calvin mimicked. " 'If you were a real magician.' " When

Jenny got into her better-than-you-real-magician secretive mode, Calvin just itched to zap the zip from her tricks.

" 'If you were a real magician,' " Calvin continued to mimic as he wandered to the magic bookshelf. Monk stood there, reading a paperback.

"Listen to this!" Monk peered closer at the tiny print. "Every magician needs a special prop—a scarf, an animal, a fan—that the audience will connect with him. This prop helps to make the magic act unique."

Monk stopped reading. "What is Jenny's special prop?"

"Plastic dog doo."

Monk searched the page earnestly. "It doesn't say anything here about plastic dog doo."

Suddenly a brilliant thought zipped through Calvin's mind. "Does that book tell you how to do magic?"

"It should," said Monk. "It's called *Beginning Magic: 101 Tricks.*"

"Can I see it?"

"Tell me what you want to learn," Monk said eagerly, "and I'll read it to you."

"Uh, no thanks," said Calvin. He flipped through the book. He read:

How to make a small object disappear.
How to make a scarf appear.
How to bake a cake in your top hat.

So *this* is how magic is made, Calvin thought, reading carefully.

"Calvin," Ms. Eva called. "Calvin! Didn't you hear me? We're going to the pet store now."

Calvin quickly reshelved the book.

"What were you reading?" Ms. Eva asked as they walked out into the cold air.

Monk piped up. "He was reading—"

"Nothing much," Calvin interrupted. Now he, too, knew how a scarf could appear from a wand and he knew how an object could disappear. He knew how to bake a cake in a top hat. But he didn't want anyone else to know that he knew. Not yet. He felt clever and secretive. This must be the way a real magician feels, he thought.

When they reached the Anderson Circle Pet Store, Calvin paused before the front window. He liked to look at the animals on display. Sometimes kittens rolled and pounced, sometimes puppies bounced and snoozed.

Today the display animals were hamsters.

In their cage, several ginger-colored hamsters curled nose-to-toes in soft balls.

"They're so round!" Jenny exclaimed.

"And small," said Calvin.

"They're as round and small as doorknobs," said Monk.

Calvin looked at Jenny.

Jenny looked at Calvin.

"They're as round as doorknobs," Jenny said slowly.

"But smaller," said Calvin.

They leaned closer to the glass.

At that very moment, one of the hamsters stretched. His yawn revealed a pink tongue and a set of long teeth. Then he tumbled over the other sleeping hamsters and scuttled to the edge of the cage. He peered up at the three humans peering in at him.

"He looks like a rabbit," said Calvin. "A rabbit with short ears and a tiny tail."

"I think he looks like a mouse," said Jenny. She shook her head doubtfully. "I'm not sure a hamster will make a good magic animal."

The hamster stood on his hind legs. He scampered over to his sleeping friends, nudged them, and scampered back. He stuck his nose through the cage bars and worked his whiskers. The wide, dark eyes in the ginger-fur face gazed straight at Calvin.

Calvin considered the animal. "This hamster," he pronounced, "is perfect."

"An animal in a magic act must be quiet and focused," said Jenny. "This hamster seems the opposite of that."

"Ah, Jenny." Calvin shook his head wisely. "Your act needs an animal with pizzazz. And believe me," he pronounced with great certainty, "this hamster has a lot of pizzazz."

"A *hamster!*" *said Ms. Eva. "Wouldn't you like a* nice fish?"

"No!" said Calvin and Jenny together.

"Ms. Eva," Jenny continued earnestly, "believe me, a fish is no good in a magic act. My mother will let me have a hamster. She just said no pet larger than a doorknob. And no mice."

"A hamster is a cousin to the mouse," Monk spoke up. "It's a rodent. Like a squirrel or a rat."

"A rat!" said Ms. Eva.

"Quiet," Calvin whispered to Monk.

"Well," said Ms. Eva, "your mother did tell me to help you pick out a good pet for your magic act. She wanted something small—"

"Hamsters are *very* small," Calvin broke in.

Jenny nodded, pointing to a sign. "And look!

They're on sale. I could buy two hamsters for the price of one."

"Never mind that," Ms. Eva said hurriedly. "I think one hamster is quite enough."

"Okay," said Jenny. "One hamster is quite enough." She fixed Ms. Eva with a pleading eye. "I promise that if my mother doesn't like this hamster, I'll bring him right back. No questions asked."

"We could name him Pizzazz," said Calvin, "and call him Zazz, for short."

"What do you mean 'we'?" said Jenny. "This hamster is going to be a trained magic animal." She gestured dramatically at the little creature, who was briskly cleaning his whiskers. "Some day this hamster—this very ordinary hamster—will be the *ultimate* magic hamster."

"Can't we play with him?"

"Only on his days off," said Jenny.

Monk had already wandered into the store and was reading a book entitled *The Care and Feeding of Your Hamster.*

Calvin could never understand Monk. Why would he want to *read* about hamsters when he was surrounded by the real, live, ginger-fur thing?

"Hey, Zazz," Calvin whispered. The hamster

took a quick break from his whisker bath and peered up at Calvin.

Jenny had already picked out a cage, a bag of cedar chips, a box of hamster food, and special training treats.

Then she saw it.

An animal with long, white fur.

An animal smaller than a rabbit and larger than a hamster.

A guinea pig.

"A guinea pig," exclaimed Jenny, "would be the perfect magic animal!"

Calvin almost fell over. How could Jenny think of buying a guinea pig when she could have this dark-eyed, intelligent, wonderful hamster?

Calvin looked at the guinea pig. He scrutinized its long, white fur. It sat calmly in its cage. It looked like a fuzzy bedroom slipper.

The guinea pig just sat. It didn't scamper or wash its whiskers or inspect its cage.

"Jenny." Calvin chose his words carefully. "This guinea pig seems boring. Very boring. No pizzazz."

Jenny smiled at the guinea pig. "Do you think so? I think it seems quiet and focused. Very focused. The right kind of animal for magic."

Calvin glanced at the window display. Pizzazz

was standing against his cage, practically *begging* Calvin to take him home.

Jenny clucked to the guinea pig, who curled up and went to sleep.

"Jenny." Calvin chose his words even more carefully. "That guinea pig is bigger than a door-knob. *Much* bigger than a doorknob."

"Not *much* bigger," said Jenny.

"That guinea pig," Calvin insisted, "is as big as *two* doorknobs. What would your mother say?"

Jenny gazed at the snoozing guinea pig. "Do you think she would notice?"

"Your mother," said Calvin, "has the eyes of a hawk."

"That's true," Jenny said sadly. "I better stick with the hamster."

What a relief, Calvin thought. He went back to examining all the hamster playthings on the shelf. If he had the money (and if his parents were less worried about re-*spon*sibility), Calvin knew he would buy Pizzazz in a minute—in a *second*—and buy all the special hamster wheels, rings, mazes, and bells that his hamster cage could hold.

Calvin picked up a hollow plastic ball with a tiny door. The label showed a picture of a hamster rolling happily inside the ball while the ball rolled across the floor.

With this ball, Calvin told Jenny, Pizzazz could really travel.

"This hamster," said Jenny, "doesn't need to travel."

As if to prove her wrong, Pizzazz chose that very moment to dash across his cage. He climbed his bars, poked his nose through, and gazed, with the curious gleam of a great explorer, at the vast jumble of dog treats and squeak toys in the world beyond.

"See?" said Calvin.

Jenny added the plastic ball to her pile. "But don't forget," she cautioned Calvin, "this is a *magic* hamster. He has a job to do."

The next morning Calvin tried to cram a knitted cap onto Monk's head. Monk kept reading.

"Monk!" Calvin exclaimed through gritted teeth. "Do you want your ears to freeze?"

Monk kept reading.

"They'll freeze like icicles and drop off. Someone will step on them. Crunch!"

Calvin pulled the cap down hard. Monk kept reading.

Monk sure lived up to his nickname, Calvin thought. Although christened Theodore Weiss Hastings, Monk had become "Monk" when he was three years old. "Look at that baby hunched over his book," Dad had said proudly. "He's like a little monk reading some ancient words. He's like a little long-ago monk guarding the knowledge of the world."

Calvin sighed. Monk might be able to guard the world's knowledge, but for today Calvin wished his brother would just guard his own ears from the cold.

Monk kept reading, his knit cap cocked at a strange angle. Calvin hustled him out the door.

And there was Jenny, hamster cage in hand.

"Calvin!" Jenny gestured tragically; the cage flew out; and the sleeping hamster rolled willy-nilly across his cedar chips. "Pizzazz is *bigger* than a doorknob."

Calvin lifted the cage gently from Jenny's gesturing hand. He looked at the hamster; he looked at the doorknob.

"Not bigger than this doorknob," he said.

"Well, he's bigger than ours. My mother made me hold Pizzazz next to our doorknob—can you believe that? And he kept stretching and squirming till he was as long as a ruler, Mom said. She said it three times: 'He's as long as a ruler.' I told her she was exaggerating."

"What did she say then?"

"She said, 'You know the rule.' "

"Oh," said Calvin.

Everyone was quiet, gazing at the snoozing hamster.

"Hey!" Calvin had a brilliant thought. "Did you tell your mother you needed Pizzazz for your magic act?"

"Yeah," Jenny sighed. "My mom said, 'Sorry, honey, you have to make him disappear.' " She crossed her arms. "Needless to say, I flat-out *refused* to laugh at that dumb joke."

Pizzazz continued to sleep, curled nose-to-toes, as round and small as a doorknob. Jenny shook her head. "Pizzazz," she said, "why didn't you do that last night?"

She turned to Calvin. "Do you think your dad? . . ."

Calvin looked down at the toes of his high-tops. He couldn't answer past the sad knot in his throat. In his head, he heard his father's speech again, with that word "re-*spon*sible" resounding three times.

"Give him to someone else," Monk spoke up suddenly. "Someone who will let us visit."

"Ms. Eva," Calvin said slowly, "would surely love a hamster."

"And it's almost Valentine's Day," said Jenny.

"I was going to make her a card, but Pizzazz is a much better gift. I'll even give her the hamster ball and food and cedar chips."

Jenny thought a moment. "Well, maybe not *give*," she said. "But I can let her *borrow* those things if she lets me train Pizzazz to be a magic hamster."

Calvin could tell Jenny liked this idea. She lost her sad look and began to gesture again. "Ms. Eva and I will be co-owners," said Jenny. "I'll train Pizzazz after school and Ms. Eva can play with him the rest of the time."

For a *co*-owner, Jenny was still acting a lot like a *total* owner, Calvin thought. But he was too relieved at the hamster's possible rescue to point this out.

Calvin, Jenny, and Monk trooped into the elevator, pressed the button, got off at the fourth floor, and trooped down the brown-carpeted hall to Apartment 419.

Ms. Eva answered their knock, glanced at her watch, and said, "You're seven hours early."

"Actually, we're twelve *days* early." Calvin stepped forward, holding out the cage like a precious gift.

"Happy Valentine's Day!" Jenny beamed.

32

Ms. Eva surveyed the sleeping hamster. "Why, that looks like Pizzazz."

"It is," said Calvin.

"I couldn't possibly take your hamster."

"Please," said Jenny, "take him."

"Such a generous gift!" said Ms. Eva. "I couldn't possibly accept it."

"Please," said Jenny. "Please, please accept."

"So, Jenny," said Ms. Eva. "You can't keep the hamster."

"Oh," said Jenny. "How did you know?"

Ms. Eva just shook her head, straightened Monk's cap, and ushered them into the living room. She lowered herself gracefully into Snuggles.

"Jenny, didn't you say yesterday that you would return Pizzazz to the pet store if your mother didn't want him?"

Jenny's eyes filled with tears.

"Ms. Eva!" Calvin broke in. "You won't even know this hamster is around. We'll feed him; we'll clean his cage. Jenny will teach him magic. I'll play with him. Shoot, you'll find yourself wondering if a hamster really *does* live in Apartment 419."

"I wonder," Ms. Eva reflected, "if I'll ever wonder that."

"You'll wonder it every day," Calvin said. "Maybe every *hour*. This is one peaceful hamster. Look at the little guy! He's as quiet as a mouse."

"He *is* a mouse."

"He's *not* a mouse," Monk explained, without looking up from his book. "He's a—"

"Cousin to the mouse," Ms. Eva sighed. "Yes, we went over that yesterday."

She glanced at the misty-eyed Jenny, the book-reading Monk, and the beseeching Calvin. Finally she glanced at the sleeping Pizzazz, who chose that very moment to yawn a huge, pink-tongued, hamster-sweet yawn.

"Okay, he can stay here"—Ms. Eva checked the delighted yells—"only, *only* if you take care of him. The first time I feed that hamster so much as one . . . one bug, out he goes."

"Hamsters eat *seeds*," Monk explained.

"If I feed that hamster anything—O-U-T."

Calvin felt joy wiggle all through him. He wanted to tell Ms. Eva something nice, something that would make *her* fill up with joy.

"Ms. Eva!" he exclaimed. "Ms. Eva, Snuggles is . . . Snuggles is . . . *beautiful.*"

"Indeed." Ms. Eva's lips twitched.

"And comfortable!" Calvin wanted to hug Ms. Eva, the hamster, even Snuggles.

"Well," said Ms. Eva, "you should certainly sit in Snuggles tonight when you do your homework."

And she gave Calvin one graceful wink.

"*Snow, snow, snow,*" *Calvin sang softly to himself.* He sat up straight on his orange bus seat and peered out the window.

The city bus rumbled and plowed through the slushy street. Cars pushed slowly past. Grown-ups stomped up the bus steps, hunched in the seats, and constantly complained, "Worst snowstorm in fifteen years."

Calvin waved to Mr. Calhoun, who was trudging in thick boots to his art gallery. He watched as Dr. Jamar, carrying a blanket-wrapped box, unlocked the door under the VETERINARIAN sign.

"Snow, snow, snow," Calvin sang. And from roofs, sidewalks, and trees, the icy snow twinkled back at him.

Another day off from school—hooray! Calvin,

Monk, and Jenny had spent the whole morning at Ms. Eva's. Monk had read, Jenny had flourished (and dropped) her magic scarves, and Calvin had trained Pizzazz—surely the smartest hamster on earth—to sit up straight in his palm and nibble sunflower seeds. Calvin had even given Pizzazz a trip in the elevator when he went down to the lobby to check Ms. Eva's mail. Pizzazz had seemed particularly interested in a thin, blue envelope and had gnawed a few holes by the stamp.

But Ms. Eva had to teach her noon dance class at the YWCA, so everyone had bundled into boots, scarves, and coats, and had caught the city bus downtown. "Maybe we can have hot cocoa with Roscoe and Alma Rae after class," Ms. Eva had suggested.

As the bus moved slowly past the snow-dazzled city, Monk read, Jenny practiced a new scarf twist, and Ms. Eva reviewed her dance ideas.

Calvin focused on one thought.

How, he kept wondering, had Ms. Eva managed to discover Pizzazz in his coat pocket right before they had left? She must be psychic, Calvin figured. She must be one of those people who can read other folks' minds. How else could she have pinpointed the exact pocket and lifted out the sleepy hamster? "He'll get cold" was all she had said. But Pizzazz, that smart, curious creature, would surely have liked the trip.

And he would have liked the dance class.

At first, Calvin had surveyed the YWCA dance floor and thought boring, boring, boring. In a corner, Monk was doing his usual Monk thing; Jenny was doing hers. Ms. Eva was flowing across the polished floor, demonstrating steps. The class members stood around in baggy sweatpants, looking awkward. They shuffled this way, they stomped that way. Roscoe and Alma Rae watched carefully from the side and offered advice.

"Relax when you jazz-walk," Roscoe suggested to one stiff woman.

"Let your shoulders roll," said Alma Rae.

Ms. Eva was very patient. She flowed again gracefully across the floor. The others followed, *almost* flowing, not quite graceful.

Calvin slumped and fidgeted. The floor was brown wood, the ceiling was fake stone. There was absolutely nothing to look at, nothing to focus on —except being bored. Even listening to Monk mumble over his book would be better than this!

"Let's try that again, this time with music," said Ms. Eva. "And just let yourself move."

She slipped a tape into the machine and stood gracefully. The other dancers panted and sagged.

Sound came out of the machine.

Whoom! That sound started pulling Calvin out of his slump. He could feel his shoulders rolling, his legs moving his boots. The tune kept repeating itself, and there was a high, bright note to lean into. *Yeah.* The other dancers felt it, too, he could tell. They danced with no stiffness, arms loose, knees working just fine. And the three dance teachers jazz-walked with style.

Calvin wished Pizzazz could feel this, dancing in his pocket. This curve into the music, this long unrolling of sound.

Suddenly the one long note rippled into many short notes. To Calvin, the sound was like a great sky breaking into pieces of blue, like a vast space breaking into thousands and millions of pieces of blue, which traveled the stale air as sweetly as rain. He could hear the rain-sound falling around him, touching his arm and his leg and his face. And, strangely, he could feel it within. Inside his belly, deep in his mind. Then he, too, was a small piece of blue, a traveling sound, and the notes went on and on.

When the tape whirred down to silence, Ms. Eva said, "Calvin, that was John Coltrane, the jazz musician, playing his saxophone. Did you like that piece?"

Calvin just nodded. He nodded and nodded.

Roscoe laughed. "Coltrane's sax had the same effect on me when I first heard it. I went all goose-kneed and couldn't speak for dreaming. I danced to his sound for years—now I just do it to keep the legs limber."

As Ms. Eva's class prepared to leave, Calvin kept hearing that blue, falling music deep in his mind. He kept seeing Ms. Eva and her two friends dancing with style.

When the last older student had left, Calvin turned to Ms. Eva, Roscoe, and Alma Rae. "That's better than any dancing on TV," he said. "You should give shows!"

Alma Rae shook her red head. "Who wants to watch some old folks dance?"

Roscoe patted his belly. "The extra weight would slow down my steps."

Ms. Eva smiled sadly. "I'm afraid Alma Rae is right. I've tried programs in the past with older dancers. We work so hard, and no one comes to watch us perform."

"No offense," said Calvin, "but maybe people don't want to watch dance. I mean," he added hastily, "they will want to watch your kind of dance once they get to the show, but they might not want to come *just* to watch dance."

Ms. Eva nodded. "You've got a point there, Calvin."

"Maybe you can invite some other people to perform, too," Calvin said excitedly. "How about a juggler and a counting pony? Even I would come to watch a juggler and a pony!"

"Well," said Ms. Eva, "a multi-arts show is a good idea, Calvin. A very good idea. But let's think carefully before we invite the juggler and the pony. We don't want our show to turn into a circus."

"Oh," said Calvin. "I was hoping we did."

"You need a poet." Monk spoke suddenly from the depths of his book.

"A poet!" said Calvin. "They're all dead."

"No," said Monk, still reading. "I'll find one."

Calvin remembered a picture of a poet in one of Monk's books. The poet had wild eyes and long, wild hair. Calvin hoped Monk wouldn't manage to find that particular poet.

"We'll have a celebration of the arts," said Alma Rae, doing a quick dance step, "for the community. Nothing too fancy. The audience can donate a little money at the door."

"We'll need to find a space for the show," said Roscoe, planning out loud. "And let's think of some other performers to invite."

Jenny came closer, flourishing her scarf.

"First, let's think of a name for our dance group," said Ms. Eva.

"How about Senior Dancers?" said Roscoe.

"Boring," said Alma Rae. "I vote for Ancient Myths."

"Ancient Myths! That makes us sound really old."

"Why don't you call yourselves Silver Threads." Monk actually looked up from his book. "You know, 'Silver threads among the gold.' That's an old song," he explained to Calvin. "I can sing—"

"That's okay," Calvin said quickly.

Jenny brandished her scarf.

Calvin considered the name Silver Threads. He looked at Ms. Eva's hair. It was streaked with silver gray. Roscoe's hair had many, many silver threads. But Alma Rae's whole head was as red as fire.

"The name won't work," he said. "Look at Alma Rae's hair."

Everyone looked. Alma Rae fingered one red curl.

"Well," she said, "I actually do have silver threads. Right now they're, um, colored by red. Maybe I can grow out a few for the show."

"Yes." Calvin nodded. "You want to be authentic."

"Can you think of any other performers who might like to be in the show?" Roscoe turned to Ms. Eva.

Jenny's scarf flapped like a sail.

"Jenny," said Ms. Eva. "I'm trying to think. Please stop flapping."

Jenny stopped. Her scarf drooped. As everyone filed out the door, she stood slumped in the middle of the floor.

Calvin poked her. "You're going to miss the bus."

Jenny didn't move. "Calvin," she said, "do you think I'm a good magician?"

"Hmmm," said Calvin. He thought of all the scarves she had dropped. . . .

"I guess," Jenny continued sadly, "I'm not good enough to be in their show."

"Maybe you should try some easier tricks," Calvin suggested kindly.

"What do you mean by that?" Jenny asked. Suddenly she didn't sound sad. She sounded mad.

"Well," Calvin said, floundering, "you do mess up a lot."

"What do you mean, 'mess up'?"

Calvin chose his words carefully. "You *have* broken a lot of wands."

"Six," said Jenny. "Six is not a lot."

"And all the scarves you drop—"

"Maybe they fall sometimes." Jenny gritted her teeth. "So what?"

Calvin tried to think fast. "Jenny!" he said. "If you practice really hard, someday your act will have . . . will have a lot of . . . of pizzazz!"

Jenny wheeled and stomped after the others. "Speaking of pizzazz," she said over her shoulder, "that hamster will be in training for two—no, *three*—hours a day, starting today."

Calvin's heart bumped down. When would he have a chance to play with Pizzazz?

"That hamster," Jenny asserted, "will become the *ultimate* magic hamster."

Calvin tried to settle into Snuggles.

He curved. Snuggles rammed his back.

He wiggled. Snuggles jammed his seat.

Around him, the room hummed with excited whispers.

Jenny was trying to teach Pizzazz how to appear and disappear. Jenny looked serious. Pizzazz looked worried. The hamster lay flat against the table. He peered up at the magic scarf, which swooped down like a hawk.

For once Monk was not reading. He was writing. As he wrote he mumbled more loudly than usual.

Ms. Eva was seated at her desk, with Roscoe and Alma Rae squinting over her shoulder.

Everyone was whispering. But, Calvin reflected,

one whisper multiplied by five people was enough noise for a shout.

If it had been difficult to focus before, now it was impossible.

Calvin shut his book and wandered over to Monk.

"Listen to this poem," Monk said. He cleared his throat three times and began:

> *What do I say?*
> *I say "hey"*
> *And you say "ho"*
> *Hey Hi Ho*
> *Together we cry—*

"*Good*-bye," said Calvin, moving away fast.

Unfortunately, Ms. Eva, Alma Rae, and Roscoe were talking in language as weird as Monk's.

"Why don't I try a high kick here," said Roscoe.

"And I'll hit the beat with my hip," suggested Alma Rae.

Calvin rolled his eyes. "Who can understand that kind of talk?" he said.

"Calvin," said Ms. Eva, "shouldn't you be doing your homework?"

Calvin understood those words. He moved away fast.

At the table, Jenny frowned in concentration. She lowered her scarf. Pizzazz's eyes bugged. Jenny lifted the scarf; the hamster had disappeared.

Suddenly Calvin saw the wiggle of whiskers and white toes at the hem of the scarf.

"Stay hidden," Jenny pleaded with the hamster.

When she lowered the scarf, Pizzazz ran out. He ran to the edge of the table, stopped, and began washing his feet.

Jenny threw down the scarf. "That hamster," she said, "has absolutely no focus."

"Maybe he's tired of learning," said Calvin.

"Tired of learning!" exclaimed Jenny. "How can he be tired of learning? He hasn't learned anything yet!"

Pizzazz climbed into Calvin's palm and sniffed for seeds. Calvin smoothed the top of the hamster's head, tracing the outline of the delicate skull beneath the ginger fur. He felt Pizzazz's breath against his finger and the tickle of that tiny nose.

"Look at how straight he sits!" Calvin said. "What a smart guy!"

Jenny snorted. "That hamster," she snapped, "is dumb."

Calvin's hand closed protectively over Pizzazz. "He is not."

"He squirms constantly," said Jenny. She gazed wistfully at the ceiling. "I wish I had that guinea pig."

"Maybe it's the magic act that's dumb," said Calvin fiercely. "Did you ever think of that?"

Jenny took a deep breath. She blew it out very slowly. "My mother says never to answer in anger," she said. "I am not angry. My magic act is not dumb. That hamster is dumb."

"Your act is dumb," said Calvin. "Dumb, dumb, dumb."

"You're just jealous," said Jenny, "because you can't do magic." She didn't even take a deep breath and blow it out. Calvin could tell she was mad.

But he was mad, too. Jenny had insulted him; she had insulted Pizzazz. She didn't deserve a pet like Pizzazz. She couldn't appreciate him. All she cared about was magic, magic, magic. What was so great about her dumb tricks?

"I can do magic," said Calvin. "Anyone can."

"Cannot."

"I read a book," said Calvin. "I know how to make a small object disappear."

"Oh," said Jenny.

"I know how to make a scarf appear."

"Oh," said Jenny.

"I know how to bake a cake in a top hat." Calvin paused, then added, "*Anybody* can do magic. The trick is not to mess up."

Jenny said nothing. She looked like she might cry.

Calvin scooped up Pizzazz and rubbed his cheek against the hamster's fur. Why did Jenny have to act so mean? She *made* me say those mean things, Calvin thought.

"So there," Calvin said uncertainly. "I am not jealous."

Jenny said nothing. She began clicking her wand very softly.

"Come on, Zazz," Calvin whispered. "I bet you're glad to get rid of that stupid magic." He tucked the hamster into the exercise ball. He closed the plastic door.

Calvin kept hearing the *click* and *whoosh* of Jenny's magic. He wished the sound was a little louder, a little happier, like the old *Click. Whoosh.*

Pizzazz rolled vigorously across the floor. The ball bumped into a chair. The hamster shifted; the ball rolled to the right.

Pizzazz looked like a creature in an outer-space bubble.

Maybe somewhere in the galaxy, Calvin thought, there lives a hamster just like Pizzazz rolling through space in a bubble.

Click, whoosh, went Jenny.

Calvin kept thinking about the hamster in space. He didn't want to hear those tiny, sad click-whooshes.

She insulted me, Calvin insisted to himself. She insulted Pizzazz. Besides, her magic *is* dumb. She always messes up.

He was sure Pizzazz was much happier traveling the floor in his ball. He listened for the little bump the ball made as it hit a chair, shifted, and moved on.

Calvin heard no little bumps.

He glanced around the room. Where *was* Pizzazz and that exercise ball?

Not by Monk's chair. Not by Jenny's chair. Not by Ms. Eva's chair.

Then Calvin saw the ball beside the door to Ms. Eva's bedroom.

The ball wasn't moving.

The ball door was open.

The hamster had disappeared.

"*You mean that mouse is loose?*" cried Alma Rae.

"The ball is empty—" Calvin began.

"It's not a mouse," Monk broke in earnestly. "It's a *hamster*, which is a cousin to the mouse."

"That's mouse enough for me," said Alma Rae. "You better find him quick." She sat in Snuggles and lifted her feet straight off the floor.

"We'll have to organize a search," said Ms. Eva. "Calvin, you and Monk look in the kitchen. Roscoe, you take the bathroom. I'll look in the bedroom. Jenny can search the living room."

"That mouse is long gone," said Roscoe.

"It's a *ham*—"

"Yes, Monk, we know." Ms. Eva glanced at Calvin's worried face. "We'll just keep searching until we find him."

Calvin made Monk open all of Ms. Eva's drawers while he searched the cupboards. He moved every single can, hoping to see Pizzazz curled up behind a tin of corn, perhaps, or a jar of string beans.

No Pizzazz.

He looked in all the corners of the kitchen, and then he looked again.

No Pizzazz.

Calvin worried that the others weren't looking very hard. Already Monk was simply peering into drawers, tossing a few spoons around, not even searching the dark corners where a hamster might hide. Ms. Eva and Roscoe were grown-ups, and grown-ups usually thought pets were nothing but extra work. And Jenny had called Pizzazz "dumb." She didn't even care about him.

"Please, Pizzazz," Calvin whispered. "Please come back."

He felt like he had been whispering that for hours—and still no Pizzazz.

"Calvin," Ms. Eva said once. "Do you want to check the mail?"

Calvin only shook his head.

Finally Ms. Eva told them that their parents had called. It was time to go home for dinner.

"I'm not hungry," said Calvin.

"If we find the hamster," said Roscoe, "we'll let you know immediately. Don't worry."

"Promise you'll look in your bed very carefully," Calvin instructed Ms. Eva. "Turn on all the lights and even look inside the pillowcase. I don't want you to squash him."

"Believe me," said Ms. Eva, "I don't want that either."

As stiff as Snuggles, Jenny marched past Calvin. "You lost him," she snarled. "You didn't lock the ball's door tightly enough."

"I did," said Calvin. "I'm sure I did."

But maybe he hadn't.

It would be his fault if Pizzazz was hungry and frightened.

Maybe his parents were right. Maybe he wasn't re-*spon*sible enough for his own pet. He couldn't even take care of someone else's.

Calvin's stomach ached.

He turned to Jenny. "He ran away," Calvin said, hoping his stomach would feel better, "because you trained him too hard."

"I know that's not true," said Jenny, "and so do you." She marched out the door.

Calvin's stomach did not feel better.

54

* * *

Calvin phoned Ms. Eva after dinner.

"No, Calvin," she said. "I did not find Pizzazz."

He phoned her again after he had finished his homework.

"Pizzazz is still missing," she said.

He brushed his teeth, washed his face, put on his pajamas. He phoned Ms. Eva.

"No Pizzazz," she said.

He brushed his teeth again. He brushed them very slowly. He brushed each tooth forty times. He phoned Ms. Eva.

"Calvin," she said, "go to bed."

And when he phoned in the morning, Pizzazz was still missing.

All day at school Calvin thought about Pizzazz.

Pizzazz would be hungry. He might be stuck behind the sofa. He might be squeaking in fear.

Did hamsters squeak? Calvin wondered. He had never actually heard Pizzazz squeak. Still, mice squeaked, and hamsters were cousins to mice. It made sense that a hamster would squeak. If Pizzazz was stuck and frightened, he would squeak.

Ms. Eva would hear his squeaks and rescue him.

But what if hamsters *didn't* squeak? They might be like rabbits. Rabbits made no noise. Pizzazz might be stuck, frightened, and *not* squeaking. Ms. Eva would never know.

Calvin worried and worried.

What if Pizzazz had somehow slipped out of Apartment 419, wandered down the brown-carpeted hall, and edged into Apartment 415?

Apartment 415 belonged to Mr. Calhoun.

And to Lump, Mr. Calhoun's orange cat. Lump had the appetite of a shark.

And what did cats eat? Mice.

And probably cousins to mice. Hamsters.

Lump, that chop-licking cat, would love to get his fat paws on Pizzazz.

Oh, Pizzazz—Calvin sent thought messages to the hamster—please don't go near Apartment 415.

Calvin was so worried he couldn't eat lunch.

In math class he couldn't even look at the board. The fractions kept growing small ears and tails. They seemed to run around like frightened mice. Or hamsters.

On his paper, instead of fractions, Calvin wrote, "Hamster Hideouts."

Where would I hide, he thought, if I were a hamster?

Calvin closed his eyes. He got into a hamster frame of mind.

He curled his hands over his belly, like Pizzazz.

He wiggled his nose, like Pizzazz.

He tried to snuggle into his desk. Pizzazz liked to snuggle. Sometimes Calvin would give Pizzazz a tissue, which the hamster would carefully shred and weave into his cedar-chip nest. Shredded paper made a soft bed.

Suddenly Calvin sat straight up. It was as if Snuggles had ramrodded his back. He became a boy again, with a boy's frame of mind.

Paper!

He should look for places in Ms. Eva's apartment where paper was stored. Pizzazz might be curled up in such a place, in a paper nest of his own making.

Under the heading "Hamster Hideouts," Calvin listed places that held paper:

1. *Notepads in Ms. Eva's desk drawer*
2. *Paper towels under the sink*
3. *Napkins in the cupboard*
4. *Toilet paper in the hall closet*

Calvin could hardly wait for school to end. He squinted at the blackboard. 1, 3, 8, 6, he read.

He stared at the 6. It curled on the blackboard. The top part was like a little tail.

That 6 looked like a hamster, tucked up and snoozing.

It was a sign. Calvin *knew* he would find Pizzazz.

Calvin pounded hard on the door to Apartment
419. No answer. He pounded again.

When Ms. Eva finally opened the door, he
dashed past her. He didn't even say hi to Jenny
and Monk. He didn't even reach for the mailbox
and apartment keys dangling from the kitchen
hook.

He consulted his list:

1. Notepads in Ms. Eva's desk drawer

Calvin pulled out the drawer. He shuffled
through the notepads, scissors, envelopes, stamps,
and paper clips. No Pizzazz.

He checked:

59

2. Paper towels under the sink

He checked:

3. Napkins in the cupboard

Nothing.

The last place to look on the "Hamster Hideout" list was the hall closet.

Please, Pizzazz, Calvin silently pleaded, please be there.

He opened the door. He had wished so hard he was almost afraid to look.

He looked on the top shelf.

Nothing.

The bottom shelf.

Nothing.

He looked into a dark corner.

There, tucked into a tuft of soft blue tissue, was Pizzazz.

At first Calvin couldn't say anything. He just wanted to look and look.

Then he lifted the sleeping hamster. "Here's Pizzazz," he called out.

Jenny and Monk pushed close.

Jenny patted and patted the hamster's head.

She seemed to have forgotten that she had called him dumb.

"Oh, that silly creature," grumbled Ms. Eva. "Look what he did to my box of tissues." Then she smiled and rubbed Pizzazz's ear.

Jenny leaned closer. "Hey, Pizzazz is breathing funny."

Calvin, Monk, and Ms. Eva leaned so close their breath ruffled the hamster's fur. Calvin listened. He heard Monk breathing. He heard Jenny and Ms. Eva breathing.

He heard Pizzazz breathing. Short, wheezing gasps.

The hamster's wheezing shook his small body. He curled listlessly in Calvin's palm.

"What's wrong with him?" Calvin asked.

"Maybe he has a cold," Ms. Eva said.

"Or lung disease," said Monk.

"Or pneumonia," said Jenny.

"Do you think he'll die?" cried Calvin.

They all looked from the hamster to Ms. Eva.

"Put him back in his cage, Calvin," Ms. Eva said gently. "Pizzazz sounds like he has a cold and needs to rest quietly. Why, tomorrow he'll be hopping around, as good as new."

"Hamsters don't hop," Monk pointed out. "Gerbils hop. Hamsters *scurry*."

"Tomorrow Pizzazz will be *scurrying*," Ms. Eva corrected herself. "Just wait and see."

Calvin placed Pizzazz in his cage. Pizzazz just sat there. He didn't dig through his food dish. He didn't nuzzle his water bottle. He didn't even try to shred the three soft tissues Calvin had draped in his chips.

Pizzazz just sat and wheezed.

"Maybe we should take him to Dr. Jamar," Calvin said. "Do you think Pizzazz needs a veterinarian?"

"Why don't you wait and see," said Ms. Eva. "If Pizzazz isn't better by tomorrow afternoon, we'll take him to the vet."

Tomorrow afternoon might be too late, Calvin worried.

For the rest of the day, he, Jenny, and Monk sat by the hamster cage. Monk didn't read; Jenny didn't practice magic; and Calvin didn't think even once of checking the mail. They shredded tissues into tiny pieces and made a soft hamster bed.

Pizzazz just sat in his tissue bed and wheezed.

When their parents phoned to tell them to come home, Calvin, Jenny, and Monk left detailed instructions for Ms. Eva.

"Call us if he's better," Jenny said, dragging out the door.

"Or worse," said Monk.

"Or just call us, please, Ms. Eva, to let us know how he's doing," said Calvin.

"I'll do that," said Ms. Eva. "But, Calvin, please, no constant phone calls like last night. Try not to worry."

But that evening Calvin worried and worried. He couldn't help it.

He worried about Pizzazz not eating, and he couldn't take one bite of his chocolate pudding.

He couldn't do his homework. Each math problem, each history question kept turning into a wheezing ball of fur.

Calvin wondered why Ms. Eva didn't call. Maybe she forgot, he reasoned. Maybe she needs to be reminded.

The more Calvin thought and worried, the more he became convinced that Ms. Eva would *want* him to call. She probably would be extremely thankful to be reminded and very sorry that she had forgotten. Yes, he should call immediately.

Ms. Eva's line was busy.

Probably the other Silver Threads had called.

They wanted to talk about dancing. How could they talk about dancing when Pizzazz was sick?

Calvin dialed again.

Ms. Eva's line was still busy.

Maybe something terrible had happened to Pizzazz. Maybe Ms. Eva was trying to call Dr. Jamar. Maybe she was planning to rush Pizzazz to the animal hospital.

Calvin dialed three more times.

Each time the line was busy.

When Ms. Eva finally answered the phone, Calvin hollered, "I'm coming to help! Don't go to the vet's without me!"

"Calvin," said Ms. Eva, "I thought I said I would call *you*."

"Oh," said Calvin. "Well, here I am."

Ms. Eva sighed. "Pizzazz is still wheezing. I just finished talking to Jenny. She's as worried as you."

"I tried not to worry," Calvin said. "I really tried."

"What happened?"

"I worried more."

"I tell you what," said Ms. Eva. "Why don't you, Jenny, and Monk come spend the night here. Bring your extra blankets and camp out in my living room. That way you can keep an eye on that poor animal."

"Great!" said Calvin. "I mean, thank you, Ms. Eva. I promise to worry very quietly."

Within an hour, Calvin, Jenny, and Monk were huddled into extra blankets on Ms. Eva's living room rug.

Out of the darkness came the sound of Pizzazz's soft, steady wheezing.

Calvin curled into his blanket like Pizzazz. He wheezed like Pizzazz. He wanted to feel what Pizzazz felt. Was the hamster in pain?

"Calvin, would you *please* quit making that weird noise," Jenny complained.

"Do I sound like a sick hamster?" Calvin asked.

"No," said Jenny. "You sound like a sick dinosaur."

Calvin wheezed a little more quietly, but still loudly enough for Pizzazz to hear. He wanted Pizzazz to know he had a friend there in the night. Calvin planned to wheeze until morning, to keep Pizzazz company.

In the morning Ms. Eva would walk them to the bus stop, and then she had to catch another bus, to teach an early dance class at the YWCA. As she had whispered good-night, Ms. Eva had said once again that Pizzazz probably only had a cold and would be feeling better soon.

But, Calvin worried, what did she mean by "soon"? To Calvin, "soon" meant immediately. But he knew that "soon" to a grown-up could mean "tomorrow" or "next week" or "next year."

What if Pizzazz was not better in the morning?

What if he was worse?

Would he have to stay all day alone and sick in Ms. Eva's apartment?

Curled in his blankets, Calvin worried and wheezed.

In the morning Pizzazz was neither better nor worse. He still huddled in his cage. He still wheezed.

"Ms. Eva!" Jenny cried as she folded her blankets. "We can't leave him alone."

"His cold has to run its course," said Ms. Eva. "He'll probably be much better when you visit him this afternoon. And if he's not, I promise that we'll take him to the veterinarian."

"Ms. Eva," Monk begged between sips of orange juice. "Can't we take him to school?"

"I can think of nothing worse for a sick hamster," explained Ms. Eva, "than a cold bus ride and a day in a noisy schoolroom."

"I agree," said Calvin.

Jenny and Monk scowled.

But Calvin had a plan.

If he couldn't bring the hamster with him . . .

He'd bring himself to the hamster.

Calvin fingered Ms. Eva's spare door key, which was attached to the mailbox key. Right after breakfast he had lifted them both from the little kitchen hook and slid them into his pocket. At first, the keys had felt no bigger than pencil stubs. Now their hard metal length seemed to fill his whole pocket.

Each time he touched them, the keys seemed to grow larger.

He hoped Ms. Eva wouldn't notice.

Jenny and Monk lingered by the hamster's cage, saying their good-byes; but Calvin had already dashed to the door. He knew the sooner he got to the bus stop, the sooner he could return to Pizzazz.

He darted down the brown-carpeted hall, punched the elevator button, impatiently punched it again.

Jenny eyed him suspiciously.

Calvin's fast-moving high-tops had him out of the elevator, on the sidewalk, and at the bus stop before Ms. Eva could even ask him to wait.

"Calvin certainly is eager to get to school," said Ms. Eva.

"Humph," said Jenny.

Finally Ms. Eva's bus arrived. As she climbed the bus steps, Ms. Eva turned and yelled down.

"You children know to get on the next bus."

"Yes'm," they called back.

"Don't get off that bus until you get to school."

"Yes'm," they chorused.

"I don't want any trouble."

"Ms. Eva," said Calvin. "Try not to worry."

"Humph," said Ms. Eva.

Calvin breathed a sigh of relief when Ms. Eva's bus had rumbled out of sight. By this time, the keys in his pocket felt as big as rulers and as heavy as stones. He had been afraid Ms. Eva would spot them.

"You're up to something," said Jenny.

"Me?" Calvin widened his eyes innocently.

Jenny fixed Calvin with one suspicious eye.

Calvin gazed at the sky. He examined his fingernails. He untied and retied his shoelaces.

He could still feel Jenny's eyes on him. In his pocket the keys felt as long as yardsticks, as heavy as lead.

Finally the bus rattled up and sputtered to a halt.

Monk mounted the steps first. Jenny followed.

Calvin watched from behind as Jenny climbed the bus steps.

As soon as his right high-top hit the first stair, Calvin made a sudden open-mouthed "O" of surprise. He clapped a hand to his head.

"I can't believe I forgot that."

Jenny sat down.

"I better go back and get it."

Jenny bounced up. "What did you forget?"

"Gotta run," Calvin hollered. "I'll catch the next bus."

As the bus pulled away, he could see Jenny shaking her head, nose pressed to the window.

Calvin turned to retrace his steps to Ms. Eva's apartment. This time he moved more slowly. The keys weighed down his whole left side. He couldn't seem to walk straight. His right leg moved freely and fast; his left leg dragged. Walk; drag; walk; drag—down the sidewalk, into the building, into the elevator, down the brown-carpeted hall.

As he turned the key in Ms. Eva's door lock, Calvin felt like a thief.

But I'm not taking anything, he consoled himself.

He pushed the door open.

Maybe I'm breaking and entering, he thought. This is a crime.

Apartment 419 seemed strangely empty without Ms. Eva, Jenny, and Monk. Calvin could hear the kitchen clock tick. In the corner Snuggles loomed like a stern presence.

"I *am* entering," Calvin mumbled to himself. "But I'm not *breaking*. The lock's not broken; the door's not broken. Nothing is broken. I'm not breaking; I'm only entering."

Calvin mumbled and mumbled, but he still couldn't quite convince himself.

"I'm doing it for Pizzazz," he said out loud.

That made him feel better.

But not much.

As he slipped into the living room, Calvin could hear Pizzazz wheezing. With his head tucked up, Pizzazz looked like one miserable ball of fur.

Calvin thought about the times he had been sick. Either Mom or Dad would stay home from work and bring him chicken noodle soup and sit by his bed.

Chicken noodle soup wouldn't help a sick hamster.

But maybe Calvin's company would make him feel better.

Calvin sat. The clock ticked. The hamster wheezed.

Calvin began to count the wheezes.

One hundred and twenty wheezes per minute.

He counted his own breaths.

Thirty breaths per minute.

That was a difference of ninety breaths! That seemed like a huge difference to Calvin. Pizzazz must be really sick.

Maybe he had lung disease.

Maybe he had pneumonia.

Maybe as the seconds ticked by and the minutes passed, Pizzazz was growing weaker and weaker.

Calvin counted the wheezes again: one hundred and twenty-four per minute.

He counted his own breaths: twenty-eight per minute.

Pizzazz was getting worse. Calvin knew there was nothing he could do to help. Mom, Dad, Ms. Eva, Jenny, Monk—no one knew anything about sick hamsters.

He would have to take the hamster to Dr. Jamar, the veterinarian.

Immediately Calvin began to feel less worried. Dr. Jamar would know exactly how to make a sick hamster feel better. Hadn't Calvin visited her waiting room many Saturdays when he was pretending to own a pet? Hadn't he seen many sick, frightened animals grow stronger and calmer there?

This time he would be visiting the veterinarian's office with a real pet, even if it wasn't his own.

"Don't worry," Calvin murmured to Pizzazz. "You'll feel better soon."

Calvin quickly lined the bottom of Pizzazz's plastic ball with tissues. Then he placed the hamster in the middle of the soft nest. Calvin wrapped the ball in a scarf to keep out any cold drafts. He pulled on his jacket and carefully locked Ms. Eva's door—he didn't want anyone else breaking and entering. As he slid the keys into his pocket, he marveled that such small things could feel so heavy. His whole left side drooped toward the ground.

The three-block walk to the vet's office was short, even with the heavy keys. The wind tore at the tassels on the scarf-wrapped plastic ball, but Calvin held on tightly. He could hear Pizzazz's muffled breathing.

A bell chimed cheerfully when Calvin pushed open the door of the vet's office. As usual, the waiting room gleamed, all clean and white; and

bright magazines covered a low red table. A crisp medicine smell filled the air.

Waiting in that light-filled room were animals of all shapes and sizes and styles.

Each animal looked worried.

Slouched on the floor, a German shepherd puppy covered its head with its paws. An English sheepdog trembled.

Calvin remembered the times he had waited for dentists and doctors who examined human patients. He remembered feeling twitchy and worried. Even though these patients were animals, Calvin could tell the feelings were the same.

"Don't worry, Pizzazz," Calvin whispered to the scarf-covered ball.

"Hello, Calvin," said a familiar voice.

It belonged to Mr. Calhoun, from Apartment 415. Mr. Calhoun balanced a black box on his knee. Through a small screen at the end of the box glared one green eye.

Calvin peered at the eye.

A low "Reee-oowww" rumbled from the box.

"What's wrong with Lump?" Calvin asked.

"I'm afraid he's not his usual perky self," said Mr. Calhoun. "I thought the vet should look at him."

Calvin glanced again at the grim green eye in

the little black box. He could think of lots of words to describe Lump. Huge. Mean. Hungry. "Perky" would not have been his first choice.

Calvin unwrapped Pizzazz. He softly tapped the plastic ball.

"*Rreeee-ooowww!*" screamed the black box.

Pizzazz flattened himself against the blue tissues. His dark eyes bugged with terror.

"I think Lump smells your mouse," said Mr. Calhoun.

"Hamster," Calvin corrected, quickly covering Pizzazz and moving to a seat far from that fierce black box. He felt relieved when the vet called Lump into the examining room.

Maybe Lump will get a shot, he thought.

Then he started worrying that Pizzazz might get a shot.

Calvin didn't know whether to feel relieved or more worried when the vet finished with Lump and called for Pizzazz.

"Why don't you stop by the art gallery some Saturday afternoon," said Mr. Calhoun as he opened the door. "We have painting classes for kids. You might like that." As Mr. Calhoun left, the door again cheerfully chimed, and the black box fiercely snarled.

Calvin had no time to think of art galleries. He

had a sick hamster on his hands. In the plastic ball Pizzazz trembled and wheezed.

"Don't worry, Pizzazz," Calvin kept murmuring. "You'll feel better soon."

In the examining room Dr. Jamar picked up the hamster and stroked him until he calmed.

Watching Dr. Jamar's kind strokes, Calvin felt calmer, too. It was almost as if Dr. Jamar were stroking *his* head and not Pizzazz's. Calvin took deep, calm sniffs of the sharp medicine smell as Dr. Jamar asked him questions.

Then Dr. Jamar examined Pizzazz. She flashed a light in his eyes and touched his belly.

"Hmmm," said Dr. Jamar.

Calvin waited for the worst.

Lung disease.

Pneumonia.

Shots.

He held his breath.

"Your hamster," said Dr. Jamar, "has a bad cold."

Calvin's breath escaped with a sigh. "A cold?"

"A cold," Dr. Jamar repeated. "Make sure you keep his cage in a warm, dry spot. For the next three days give him a few drops of cod-liver oil on a small piece of bread. He should be feeling better in no time."

"No shot?" asked Calvin.

Dr. Jamar smiled. "Just cod-liver oil. You can buy it at the drugstore."

Calvin barely felt the floor beneath his high-tops. Relief had him floating like a cloud. Even those heavy keys couldn't bring him down. He wrapped Pizzazz back up in his ball and scarf.

"How do you want to pay?" Dr. Jamar asked.

"Pay?" Calvin asked. His floating mood dipped a little.

"Do you want to pay now?" said Dr. Jamar. "Or should I send you a bill?"

"Oh," said Calvin airily, "just send me a bill."

"I need your address," said Dr. Jamar. Her sharp-pointed pen hovered over her pad.

Calvin's floating mood took a nosedive. His whole body felt heavy. Very slowly he gave an address.

He gave Ms. Eva's address.

Hopefully Ms. Eva would understand. If the bill was sent to Calvin at his address, his parents would know he had skipped school. He would be in *big* trouble.

Surely Ms. Eva would understand. After all, Pizzazz lived with Ms. Eva. She wouldn't want him to be sick. And, Calvin reasoned, by the time the bill came to Ms. Eva's apartment, he would have figured out a way to pay it. After all, how much could it cost to poke a hamster—a very small animal—and recommend cod-liver oil?

Pizzazz will be better in a few days, Calvin comforted himself. That knowledge was worth any amount of money.

Calvin bought the cod-liver oil and trudged back to his apartment building. He wondered about that bill. Would it be ten dollars? Twenty dollars? Thirty dollars?

Where would he get thirty dollars? Calvin worried.

Still worrying, he dragged himself to the elevator, pushed the button, and rode to the fourth floor.

Cradling the scarf-wrapped plastic ball, Calvin inserted the key into the door of Apartment 419.

"Almost home, Pizzazz," he murmured. At that moment he decided he would tell Ms. Eva about the vet bill and ask for her advice.

The lock clicked. He turned the knob.

"Why, Calvin," came Ms. Eva's voice, "what are you doing here?"

Grounded.

No TV, no phone calls, no dessert for three weeks.

No leaving the apartment building after school.

Six days had passed since Ms. Eva had caught Calvin entering her apartment. He still had fifteen days of being grounded.

No TV, no phone calls, no dessert. No leaving the apartment building after school.

Spine wedged hard against Snuggles, book open to the first page of chapter two, Calvin thought about the events leading to his grounding. His memories were like a wide-awake nightmare.

He remembered how perfectly the door key had fit into the lock. He remembered the neat click.

He remembered thinking that soon he could

place the heavy keys back on the kitchen hook. What a relief! He remembered thinking he would tell Ms. Eva about the vet's bill.

He remembered Ms. Eva's voice: "Why, Calvin, what are you doing here?"

That was the worst part.

He remembered Ms. Eva's surprise, then her disappointment.

The words had stuck in his throat when he told her the story. Somehow he had left out the part about the vet's bill coming to her address.

And then Ms. Eva had taken the two keys. She did not hang them from the kitchen hook. She hid them.

No more checking the mail.

It wasn't so much checking the mail that Calvin missed. He missed Ms. Eva's trusting him. Checking the mail was only part of that. These days, the blue envelopes, postcards, and bills spread across Ms. Eva's desk all carried a faint air of disappointment.

These days, Calvin often sat in Snuggles. Even that hard chair couldn't make him feel worse. He listened to Pizzazz sniffling in his cage. At least the hamster was feeling better.

Calvin had been worried that Ms. Eva might

get rid of Pizzazz, might return him to the pet store.

"No, Calvin," Ms. Eva had said. "I won't use Pizzazz to punish you."

That made Calvin feel better—and worse.

Ms. Eva didn't treat him any differently. She just didn't let him check the mail.

And somehow—Calvin couldn't figure out why —that made him feel worse than Dad's lectures or Mom's grounding.

Calvin shifted in Snuggles and sighed. Alma Rae, Roscoe, Jenny, and Monk had gone off to the thrift shop to find costumes for the Silver Threads. At her desk, Ms. Eva made phone call after phone call, trying to find a good place for a show.

Each theater or auditorium wanted money to rent the space. Lots of money.

"Oh, something will turn up," Ms. Eva would say airily whenever Monk or Jenny or one of the Silver Threads would ask.

At this rate, they would be dancing in the street.

An excited *tat-tat-tat* at the door made Calvin look up from Snuggles's grim depths. In burst the Silver Threads, Jenny, and Monk. They upended their thrift-shop bags, and a bright mess of scarves, belts, skirts, and beads littered the floor. Jenny dashed into the bathroom and strolled out a minute later wearing a kid-sized tuxedo and a black top hat.

Everyone clapped as she bowed.

Looking shyly pleased, Jenny clicked her wand and—*whoosh!*—a scarf appeared.

"Encore! Encore!" Roscoe hollered.

Jenny flourished her wand again. She did every single one of her magic tricks, even the first-time-ever disappearing hamster act.

For once Jenny did not mess up. The wand did not break, the scarf did not fall, the hamster did not run away. Jenny looked as surprised as Calvin felt.

"Jenny," Ms. Eva called out as she clapped, "you should be in our show."

"I don't know. What if I mess up?"

"That was perfect! You're not going to mess up."

That was easy for Ms. Eva to say, Calvin thought. He knew how easy it was to mess up—even if you were trying very hard *not* to mess up.

But Ms. Eva wouldn't take Jenny's no for an answer. "My dear," she said, "you just have to *believe* you can do it."

Jenny did not look convinced.

"I thought you wanted to be a magician and perform before an audience."

"I do," said Jenny.

"Well, here's your big chance."

Jenny did not look pleased with her big chance. In fact, she looked worried. Calvin knew that worried feeling. These days, it seemed all he felt was worry. First Pizzazz getting lost, then getting sick. Now the vet's bill. . . . He still hadn't told Ms. Eva about that vet's bill. He didn't want to see her disappointed look again.

"And we have a poet," Monk said. "Alfred Ludlott came—"

"*The* Alfred Ludlott?" Roscoe broke in.

"*The* Alfred Ludlott," Monk replied, looking pleased with himself. "He came to my class and I asked him—"

"Wait a minute," Calvin interrupted. "Why would a poet come to your class?"

"To talk about his work," said Monk. "Sometimes a basketball player comes, or a football player. Why not a poet?"

"I'd rather have a basketball player," said Calvin.

Monk continued raptly, "Alfred Ludlott reads his poetry out loud at schools. He reads it out loud in bookstores and colleges and theaters. He says that poetry belongs *everywhere*."

"It does not," said Calvin. "It belongs in books."

"And," continued Monk as if he hadn't heard, "Alfred Ludlott says that poetry belongs to *everyone*."

"Everyone?"

"Everyone."

"Well," said Calvin, "I don't want it."

"Me neither," said Jenny.

Ms. Eva broke in. "Why would Alfred Ludlott want to read his poetry at our community show? Does he know we can't pay him?"

Monk simply repeated, "Alfred Ludlott says poetry belongs everywhere and to everyone."

"For free?" asked Ms. Eva.

Monk nodded vigorously. "He is"—Monk paused for effect—"a great man."

He is a kook, Calvin thought.

Monk continued, "Alfred Ludlott said he would be honored—he even used that word 'honored'—to read his poems at our show. But he can only read in April. After that he leaves for a long book tour."

"But this is March," said Ms. Eva.

"I told him the show was April eleventh."

"But we don't have a place to give a show!"

Monk looked accusingly at Ms. Eva. "He needed a date. And you kept saying, 'Oh, a place will turn up.'"

"It will," said Ms. Eva. "But maybe not precisely on April eleventh."

"It would be a shame"—Monk paused—"if Alfred Ludlott couldn't be at our show."

"Yes," said Ms. Eva. "But I've made seventeen phone calls. I don't know if I can find a place by April eleventh."

"Ms. Eva," said Monk, "you just have to *believe* you can do it."

"Oh," said Ms. Eva.

"I thought you wanted to give a show," said Monk, "with the Silver Threads and other performers."

"I do," said Ms. Eva.

"Alfred Ludlott—*the* Alfred Ludlott—said he would be honored to be in our show on April eleventh. Ms. Eva, this is your big chance."

Ms. Eva did not look pleased with her big chance. In fact, she looked worried.

These days after school, Calvin walked as slowly as he could from the bus stop to the apartment building. Then he walked even more slowly from the big door to the elevator. In the elevator he would count slowly to 100 before he pushed the button that would take him to the fourth floor, to Apartment 419.

Why move fast? he'd think, as he lollygagged from the bus stop to the door to the elevator. There was nothing to look forward to but the day's long last hours, full of being grounded.

No TV, no phone calls, no dessert.

No leaving the apartment building after school.

Calvin knew what he would find each day when he slowly opened the door to Apartment 419.

Roscoe and Alma Rae would be deep into their Silver Threads steps. Some jazz, turned low, would be working the air, and one long sax note would sound. Monk would be writing and reciting, reciting and writing, as if *he* were Alfred Ludlott. Pizzazz would be locked into Jenny's rigorous magic training schedule. And Ms. Eva would be making her thousandth phone call to some theater or auditorium, which would have no space—absolutely nothing—on April 11.

Calvin had nothing to look forward to but the slow walk across Ms. Eva's living room to Snuggles. There, gripped in Snuggles's grim arms, he would open his book, begin his homework, and try not to watch Jenny training Pizzazz.

He knew how he would feel sitting in Snuggles. He would feel left out and lonely.

Why move fast, he'd think each day, to get to a place just to feel sad?

Sometimes he'd count to 200 before he'd push the elevator button.

This was one of those days.

Calvin was standing inside the elevator with the door open. He had counted to fifty-nine.

"Hello, Calvin." Mr. Calhoun stepped into the elevator.

"Hey," said Calvin. Sixty-one, he counted.

"Lovely day," said Mr. Calhoun.

"Hmmm," said Calvin. Sixty-four.

"Just coming home to pick up some papers."

Calvin counted.

Mr. Calhoun waited.

The elevator door stood open.

"Should I push the button?" Mr. Calhoun asked.

"No!" said Calvin. He had only counted to ninety-three.

"Okay," said Mr. Calhoun. He waited. He cleared his throat. "You should, um, stop by the art gallery soon," he finally said.

"Hmmm," said Calvin, trying silently to keep counting.

Mr. Calhoun continued to chat. "We took out a wall and opened up a big space."

"Hmmm," said Calvin.

Mr. Calhoun smiled, thinking of his big space. "There's enough room now for an elephant to dance the tango."

"Did you say *dance*?" asked Calvin.

"Yes." Mr. Calhoun looked surprised. "Why do you ask?"

But Calvin was thinking, If there's enough room for an elephant to dance the tango, surely there's enough room for three Silver Threads to dance their jazz thing.

"Mr. Calhoun," said Calvin. "We have to talk."

Standing in the elevator with the door open, Calvin told Mr. Calhoun about the Silver

Threads. He mentioned Pizzazz, the magic hamster. He talked about a community show with other performers.

"All we need," Calvin finished, "is a place on April eleventh."

"Hmmm," said Mr. Calhoun. "I'm not sure I can help. My place may be too small. I might not have enough chairs—"

"Did I mention," Calvin broke in, "that Alfred Ludlott will be reading his poems?"

"*The* Alfred Ludlott?" asked Mr. Calhoun.

"None other," said Calvin.

"Well," said Mr. Calhoun. He looked at the ceiling of the elevator; he looked at his shiny shoes; he looked at Calvin.

"*The* Alfred Ludlott?" he repeated.

Calvin nodded.

"Why would Alfred Ludlott read his poems at your community show when he has given readings at colleges and expensive theaters? Why, he's even traveled to other countries and his readings have sold out!"

"Well," said Calvin, hoping his explanation would not sound too dumb, "Alfred Ludlott says that poetry belongs everywhere—and to everyone."

"For free?" asked Mr. Calhoun.

"For free," replied Calvin.

91

"Ah," said Mr. Calhoun raptly. "Alfred Ludlott is a great man."

"So I've been told," said Calvin.

Mr. Calhoun stepped out of the elevator. "Calvin," he said. "Why don't you come look at the gallery? If you think the space is right for your show, we can talk about details."

Calvin stepped out of the elevator, too.

A voice in his head kept nagging, *No leaving the apartment building after school. No leaving. . . . No leaving. . . .*

Calvin squashed down that voice. This was his big chance. He could find a place for Ms. Eva so she wouldn't look worried. He could do something for the show so he wouldn't feel left out.

He followed Mr. Calhoun out the apartment building door.

"The Alfred Ludlott." Mr. Calhoun smiled and smiled.

Calvin liked the big space. He liked the bright paintings on the walls. He liked Mr. Calhoun's asking for his advice.

"Should the chairs be lined up this way?" Mr. Calhoun asked.

"Yes," said Calvin.

"Do we want bright lights or dim lights?"

"We need one spotlight," said Calvin.

Calvin felt very important. He gave advice freely. He and Mr. Calhoun planned for a wonderful performance on April 11.

Then Calvin remembered one detail that had worried Ms. Eva.

"Mr. Calhoun," he asked, "how much money do you want for this space?"

Mr. Calhoun thought. He looked at the ceiling; he looked at his shiny shoes; he looked at Calvin.

Finally he said, "It will be so interesting to hear Alfred Ludlott read his poems that I won't charge you a cent."

Calvin felt both relieved and surprised. He personally would have been more interested in the magic hamster act, but Mr. Calhoun preferred *poems*. This Alfred Ludlott must be pretty famous. Calvin began to feel curious about him.

Mr. Calhoun walked Calvin to the door of the art gallery. He shook Calvin's hand.

"I hope Lump is feeling better," Calvin said.

"The vet said he was lonely," said Mr. Calhoun. "I've started bringing him to work with me." Mr. Calhoun pointed to a basket under a picture of yellow tulips. "I think he's back to his old perky self."

Calvin looked in the basket. Lump was sleeping. The tip of his tail twitched. Even in sleep he looked mean and hungry.

"And how is your hamster feeling?" Mr. Calhoun asked.

"He's much better," Calvin said, "but he's not really *my* hamster."

"I thought—"

"I wish that he *was* my hamster," Calvin said. "But he's not."

After shaking hands again, Calvin wandered back to his apartment building. Two feelings kept weaving in and out of his thoughts. One minute he'd feel pride at having found a place for April 11. Ms. Eva, Jenny, Monk—everyone would be happy. He'd be a hero! The next minute—*thump!*—all his happiness squashed down to sadness. He wished Pizzazz belonged to him. He wished the ultimate magic hamster was just Calvin Hastings's ordinary, ginger-fur hamster to visit and feed and hold.

Head down, Calvin lollygagged down the street. His thoughts swung back and forth between happy and sad.

Suddenly he stopped.

Those shoes coming toward him looked very familiar.

The shoes stopped.

Calvin looked up.

"Calvin," said Dad, "what are you doing here?"

If there was anything worse than being grounded, Calvin reflected, it was being double-grounded. He wedged his back against Snuggles.

No TV, no phone calls, no dessert. No leaving the apartment building after school.

For four weeks. Four long weeks.

In the next room Ms. Eva, Roscoe, and Alma Rae practiced their dance steps. Jazz riffed through the apartment and made Calvin's high-tops twitch. Monk was hard at work, writing a poem, while Jenny flicked her scarves. Pizzazz was hunched up, wearing a ruff.

Pizzazz hated that ruff. He tried to scratch it off. He tried to bite it off. Finally he just sat in his cage and sulked. The ruff furled around him like a flower.

Everyone was busy but Calvin. Sure, he had been showered with thanks for getting Mr. Calhoun's place. Why, he had even been double-grounded to get that place! But now his work for the show was over.

Calvin had nothing to do but be double-grounded and lonely.

The next day when he sat in Snuggles, Calvin had a different thought: If there was anything worse than being double-grounded, it was being triple-grounded. Triple-grounded and lonely.

The vet's bill had finally appeared in Ms. Eva's mail.

When Ms. Eva had shown the bill to him, all Calvin could say was "Oh." In the excitement of getting the place for the show, Calvin had forgotten about the bill.

And here it was.

Forty dollars to poke a hamster and recommend cod-liver oil.

Forty dollars!

And because Calvin had taken the hamster to the vet without first talking to Jenny or Ms. Eva (the co-owners), his parents agreed that Calvin should pay the bill. They had worked out a careful system of chores for Calvin: sweeping floors, making beds, emptying trash. Calvin would get paid for these chores and he would repay his parents, who had paid the vet's bill.

It all seemed very complicated to Calvin, but his parents were satisfied with the arrangement.

Sitting in Snuggles, Calvin reflected on his problems: triple-grounded, lonely, and in debt. It didn't seem fair to spend all this money for a pet he didn't even own.

But as he watched the hamster gnaw his perky ruff, Calvin felt that somehow Pizzazz was worth all the trouble.

"Pizzazz," Jenny called out, "stop that! You're destroying your costume."

Jenny brought the hamster to Calvin and flopped down beside Snuggles.

"I don't know if Pizzazz has what it takes to be a magic animal," she worried.

Calvin unsnapped the ruff and let Pizzazz burrow up his sleeve. He liked the tickle of whiskers against his wrist.

"What if Pizzazz messes up?" Jenny continued. "Sometimes he does well, but at other times he won't pay attention. The show is only eight days away and I don't know if he's learned anything!"

Calvin opened his mouth to defend Pizzazz. Then he snapped it shut.

If Pizzazz couldn't learn to be the ultimate magic hamster, maybe Jenny wouldn't want him.

Maybe she would sell Pizzazz.

And he, Calvin, could buy the hamster.

While he was doing all these chores to pay for that forty-dollar vet bill, Calvin figured he could sweep a few more floors, make a few more beds, and empty a few more trash cans. He could earn enough money to buy Pizzazz.

In his head Calvin heard that word "responsible." Re-e-e-e. *Spon*sible. Like a door creaking, then banging shut. Well, it wouldn't bang shut this time, he decided. He would be so responsible he would define the very word "responsible." He would never complain about any chore. He would focus, focus, focus on earning the money to buy Pizzazz. And when he had proved that he was responsible, was very, *very* responsible, surely his parents would see that he could take excellent care of a pet.

The whole process might take a long time. It might take a very long time. He might be an old man with a grizzled hamster on his knee.

But Pizzazz would belong to him.

Calvin thought about a plan. "If I were you," he said to Jenny, "I would be worried. I would be *very* worried."

"You would?" Jenny said, worried.

Calvin nodded. "Sometimes Pizzazz doesn't seem very . . . focused. You never know what he will do."

"That's true," said Jenny, looking more worried. "He appears when he should disappear, and disappears when he should appear."

Calvin heaved a big, fake sigh. "I don't know if he has what it takes to be a magic animal. If I were you," he repeated, "I would be very, *very* worried."

"I am," said Jenny. "I don't want to mess up before that big audience." Her brow furrowed as she glanced anxiously at Pizzazz.

She looked so worried that Calvin had to look away. He stared down at the yellow ruff in his hand. He stared at Jenny's slightly crooked stitches. Ms. Eva had shown Jenny how to make that ruff, and Calvin remembered Jenny's poking the stiff felt with a needle, poking her fingers, gritting her teeth. . . . She kept sewing big messy stitches, tearing them out, sewing again until she got those stitches right. It had taken her three days to attach the purple rickrack to the hem.

Calvin swallowed. "You never know what Pizzazz will do," he repeated. "And look! He's bitten a hole in his ruff."

100

"Okay, Pizzazz." Jenny scooped up the burrowing hamster. "Time to get back to work."

Jenny still looked worried on April 11, the night of the show. She let Calvin carry Pizzazz in his plastic ball.

"My hands are shaking," she said. "I don't want to drop him."

Calvin wanted to say something nice, to tell her that she would do fine and that Pizzazz would be the best, the *ultimate* magic hamster. But he didn't want to ruin his own plan. If Jenny thought Pizzazz was good at magic, she wouldn't want to sell him.

Calvin straightened Jenny's top hat. "Well," he said, "at least you *look* like a magician."

"Thanks for the compliment," said Jenny. "At least I *think* it's a compliment." But she didn't even look mad—just worried.

Calvin held up the plastic ball so that Pizzazz could see the art gallery. Metal seats were arranged neatly around the open floor space. Mr. Calhoun handed out programs to people entering the art gallery. "Welcome! Welcome!" he cried.

Lump glared from his basket.

"Alfred Ludlott," people murmured. "Where is Alfred Ludlott?"

Calvin's parents arrived and waved to him. Dr. Jamar smiled. Buster, the owner of the magic shop, gave Jenny the thumbs-up sign for good luck.

"I don't want Buster to see me mess up," Jenny whispered.

Calvin said nothing.

"Calvin," said Jenny, "do you think Pizzazz will do okay?"

Calvin shrugged. He couldn't look at Jenny's anxious face. He couldn't look at Pizzazz cradled in his plastic ball. He said nothing.

Looking worried, Jenny went off to find Ms. Eva, who was in a small room with the other Silver Threads. They were warming up before the performance.

Monk pushed his way through the crowd. He led a tall, gangling man with a few tufts of gray hair. The man held a small girl by the hand.

"This," said Monk, beaming, "is Alfred Ludlott."

"*The* Alfred Ludlott?" Calvin asked.

"None other," said Monk.

Calvin scrutinized Alfred Ludlott. He surveyed the man from the tips of his wispy hair to the tops of his scuffed brown shoes. Calvin was very disappointed. *This* was a poet? This guy looked like a bewildered bird.

Calvin hoped the big crowd wouldn't be too disappointed.

Alfred Ludlott introduced his granddaughter Lola. She was four years old and wore a jumper printed with pink bunnies. Her wide, dark eyes gazed at everything.

She reminded Calvin of someone.

Lola Ludlott turned her curious gaze to the plastic ball in Calvin's hand.

"Mouse," she said.

"Hamster," Calvin corrected.

"Hamster," she repeated.

Lola reached up to hold the ball. Calvin helped her sit down and hold the ball in her lap.

"Hamster," she said.

Suddenly Calvin realized who Lola Ludlott reminded him of.

With her wide, dark eyes and curious gaze, the granddaughter of Alfred Ludlott, the famous poet, reminded him of Pizzazz.

At that moment a lady swirled up in a sweep of black coat, hugged the bewildered Alfred Ludlott, and gushed, "What *is* that adorable animal? A rabbit?"

"Hamster," said Lola.

The lady peered closer. She stepped back. "A mouse!"

"Hamster," said Lola. She held the ball high so that the lady could get a good look at what obviously was neither a rabbit nor a mouse.

The lady did not seem pleased to examine Pizzazz at such close range. She swirled off again.

Calvin turned back to Alfred Ludlott and Monk. Monk was happily reciting his "Hey Ho" poem. Oh, no, Calvin thought. He hoped Alfred Ludlott wouldn't feel obliged to recite.

Jenny pushed up to them. "Mr. Calhoun is almost ready to start the show," she said, and rubbed her palms on her tuxedo jacket. "I'm so nervous my hands are sweating." She looked around. "Hey, where's Pizzazz?"

"Lola has him," said Calvin.

He looked down at the little girl. She gazed up with those big, dark, hamster-sweet eyes.

He looked at her lap.

There was the plastic ball.

The door was open.

The ball was empty.

Lola Ludlott held out the empty ball. "Hamster," she said. "Hamster gone."

Pizzazz had disappeared.

The news was like a nightmare to Calvin.

A nightmare that had happened before.

Only this time the nightmare was worse. Pizzazz was lost in a gallery filled with high heels, heavy boots, and hip-hopping tennis shoes. There were a hundred busy feet that could squash a hamster, a hundred nooks and crannies where a hamster could hide.

And there was Lump.

Lump's flat nose stuck over his basket. Eyes gleaming, the cat turned his big orange head from side to side. His nose worked.

He's testing the air, Calvin thought anxiously. He smells hamster.

Jenny knelt beside Lola Ludlott. "Where is the

hamster?" Jenny said each word very slowly and very clearly.

The little girl looked back at Jenny. She said very clearly, "Hamster."

"Where . . . is . . . the . . . ham . . . ster?" Jenny repeated.

"Ham . . . ster," said the little girl very slowly. "Ham . . . ster . . . gone."

"Poor Pizzazz." Jenny was almost crying. "He must be so scared. Imagine getting lost in this place."

Calvin only nodded. He felt like crying, too.

Monk and the famous poet were down on their hands and knees, hunting for the hamster in a jungle of chair legs. Soon the Silver Threads joined them and searched all corners and trash cans.

"Zazz," Calvin called softly. "Here, Zazz."

"Ouch," said Alfred Ludlott, bumping his head on a metal chair seat. He rubbed his wispy hair. "Calvin, I don't see your hamster anywhere."

"He's not really *my* hamster—" Calvin began.

"Hamster gone," Lola said. She clenched her hands tightly in her lap.

Calvin looked more closely at Lola. He looked again at her lap. One of the large pockets in her pink-bunny jumper seemed to be moving.

Lola clutched the moving pocket. "Hamster *gone*," she asserted.

Calvin pounced.

He lifted Lola's fingers away from her pocket.

Out poked a ginger-fur head.

"Hamster!" exclaimed Lola.

Calvin scooped up Pizzazz.

Lola peered into her pocket. "Hamster gone," she said sadly.

Pizzazz closed his eyes as Calvin stroked his back. Despite his sudden disappearance, the hamster seemed quite calm. He began to wash his feet as Jenny rubbed his ears.

"You sure had us worried, Pizzazz," Jenny said.

"Why were you worried?" Calvin asked quickly. "Because you wouldn't be able to do your magic act without Pizzazz?"

"Of course not," said Jenny, smoothing the top of the hamster's head. "I didn't want him to get hurt. Lump was looking awfully hungry."

"Ladies and gentlemen, please take your seats," Mr. Calhoun called. "Tonight's performance is about to begin."

"Calvin, I'm scared," Jenny whispered as Calvin settled Pizzazz in her palm. Her fingers trembled as she straightened the hamster's ruff.

"Don't worry." Calvin swallowed. "Pizzazz will be a great magic hamster."

"Do you think so?"

"I know so," said Calvin. He gently straightened Jenny's top hat. "Hey, your costume looks good. You really do look like—I mean, you *are* a real magician."

"Yeah?"

"Yeah."

And Jenny performed like a real magician. She made scarves bloom like brilliant poppies. Coins appeared from nowhere and cards fanned as perfectly as peacock tails.

Pizzazz was a credit to performing hamsters everywhere. His small ears perked; his dark eyes glowed; his ginger fur shone under the spotlight. He didn't even squirm when Jenny made him vanish—*poof!*—into a flowered scarf and turned him into a rose.

Calvin sat beside Lola Ludlott. The little girl never took her eyes off the performing hamster. Occasionally she would poke her finger into her pocket, now empty, and look sad.

"What a delightful little rabbit!" exclaimed a woman behind them.

"Hamster," corrected Lola.

When Jenny and Pizzazz finished their magic act, the crowd clapped. And clapped. And clapped. The noise sounded like thunder.

But Calvin barely noticed. He was too busy adding his own loud clapping to the thunder sound.

At first Jenny looked surprised at the applause. Then she looked shyly pleased. Then she grinned. She grinned and bowed and bowed.

Pizzazz took the applause as his due. He stood with quiet dignity in Jenny's cupped palm and gazed over his ruff at the crowd.

The Silver Threads took the floor next. Ms. Eva, Alma Rae, and Roscoe looked elegant in black leggings and long white shirts. With their gray-streaked hair, Ms. Eva and Roscoe fit their dance group's name perfectly, and even Alma Rae's red head shone with a few authentic silver threads.

When the first sax notes perked the still air, Roscoe did a slow jazz slide to the right. John Coltrane's music filled the dance space. There was that one long note Calvin loved, and then the shower of sound, note after note, washing the air, rinsing it clean. Ms. Eva's arms rose and fell, rose and fell, like the wings of a bird in a beautiful rain.

110

Calvin could tell the crowd liked what they saw. People nodded and swayed in their seats as the music moved them.

Even Lola managed to tear her gaze away from Pizzazz to watch Ms. Eva's graceful high kicks. And when Alma Rae finished, kneeling on one knee—the crowd roared.

"Silver Threads!" one man shouted. "Weave some more of those fine dance steps."

The Silver Threads did another short number before clearing the floor for the poet.

Calvin was worried about Alfred Ludlott. Under the spotlight the poet looked very wispy and very bewildered. Jenny and the Silver Threads had been showered with wild applause, but would this crowd—would anyone except Monk—really like *poems?*

Alfred Ludlott rattled his few pages.

He cleared his throat.

Calvin wiggled in his seat. The metal back felt as hard as Snuggles. Calvin decided he would clap very loudly for Alfred Ludlott, even if no one liked his poems.

Then Alfred Ludlott let his voice roll out. His voice rolled over his well-chosen words.

His voice rolled like a brown river, rolled like the deep rhythm of drums, rolled like thunder on a city-hot day. His words were not just words, they were sound—and the sound was a perfect music.

If only Monk could learn to do *that*, Calvin thought, he would be some kind of poet.

When Alfred Ludlott stopped, gulped, and smoothed back his frizzy hair, the crowd sat in stunned silence.

Alfred Ludlott spoke: "I'd like to introduce Monk Hastings tonight and thank this young friend for inviting me here. Monk, come on up and read some of your work."

Monk trotted up and shyly shook Alfred Ludlott's hand. Then with a slight squeak, he launched into his "Hey Ho" poem.

> *What do I say?*
> *I say "hey"*
> *And you say "ho"*
> *Hey Hi Ho*
> *Together we cry*
> *Ho Hey Hi*
> *Talkin' high*
> *Talkin' low*
> *Speakin' fast*
> *Speakin' slow*
> *Down the street*
> *We walk and know*

That I'll wave "hi"
And you'll say "ho"
Ho Hey Hi
Hey Hi, Hey Ho

That poem didn't sound half bad, Calvin thought.

In fact, it sounded good. He liked all the rhymes bouncing off one another. He liked the quick beat. The poem moved fast, like kids playing basketball. The words didn't so much make sense as they made sound, a sound that got deep inside, bounced around, made you smile. Funny he hadn't noticed that before, and he must have heard Monk's poem a thousand times.

The crowd liked the poem, too. They clapped their approval.

And, leaning back in his metal chair, clapping and approving with the rest, Calvin heard *his* name.

"Calvin Hastings," said Alfred Ludlott, "also deserves special thanks. The spotlight could shine on us tonight because he made it shine."

Huh? Calvin thought. What's he talking about?

"Calvin's focused attention on this show got us this lovely space," Ms. Eva added. "Thank you, Calvin."

Did she say "focused"? Calvin wondered.

"He saved this hamster's *life*"—Jenny flourished the plastic ball—"when Pizzazz was *wheezing* to death!"

Calvin squirmed. Jenny might be acting a little *too* dramatic. Still, he liked what she'd said. She made him sound like a hero!

Calvin craned his neck to find his parents in the audience. He sure hoped they were listening hard to all these nice words. Maybe they'd let up a bit on the triple-grounding.

Alfred Ludlott rolled out a few more choice words: "responsible," "hardworking," "kind."

Then it was Calvin's turn to trot up to the front and shake Alfred Ludlott's hand. He was hugged by all the Silver Threads and twice by Ms. Eva.

Calvin didn't even mind the hugs, he was that surprised.

He looked out at the audience. His parents waved. Dr. Jamar smiled broadly. Buster, the magic shop owner, gave him two thumbs up, and Mr. Calhoun winked. Even Lump looked slightly less ferocious.

The applause went on and on.

The applause was nice, but later that evening Calvin got something nicer.

* * *

Jenny and her mother, Monk, Mr. and Mrs. Hastings, and all the Silver Threads were sitting in Ms. Eva's apartment. Sipping ginger ale, they relived all the best parts of the entire show.

Calvin sat on a soft cushion, far away from Snuggles. He sniffed his ginger ale. He liked the way the bubbles tickled his nose.

"Calvin," said Ms. Eva. *"Calvin."*

"Oh," said Calvin. "I guess I was focusing."

"Calvin," Ms. Eva repeated. "I have a surprise for you."

"Great," said Calvin. A ginger ale bubble tickled his nose. He sneezed.

When he looked up, he saw Pizzazz's cage. Inside, the hamster was busy constructing a nest.

"Why, if it isn't the magic hamster," said Calvin. "The *ultimate* magic hamster."

There was still a part of him—a very small part —that wished Pizzazz had not performed *quite* so well at the show. Jenny would never want to sell such a fine hamster. So Pizzazz could never become Calvin's pet, Calvin's warm buddy to visit and feed and hold.

Calvin shook off these thoughts. Zazz and I are buddies already, he thought. Nothing can change that.

116

Dad said, "You certainly have been very responsible lately."

"And hardworking," said Mom.

"Don't forget focused." Calvin grinned.

Jenny solemnly removed a pillowcase from the top of a large cage in the corner.

"Calvin," she said. "Meet Blackstone."

Something peered out at Calvin. It sat calmly in its cage. It had long white fur.

It looked like a fuzzy bedroom slipper.

"My new guinea pig," said Jenny. "I named her Blackstone, after the famous magicians, father and son. Both Blackstones were very elegant and created the grandest, the *ultimate*, illusions. Disappearing camels, levitating ladies! Their pictures are in all the magic books: Blackstone Senior, with a black mustache; Blackstone Junior, with a neat black beard."

Calvin scrutinized the guinea pig, who curled up and went to sleep. The guinea pig did not look one bit like her namesakes.

"My mother gave me Blackstone," Jenny crowed, "even though she's bigger than *two* doorknobs—"

"I wrote a poem in honor of the occasion," Monk broke in. "Do you want to hear it?"

Calvin looked from the guinea pig to Jenny to Pizzazz. "Wait a minute—"

But Roscoe was topping everyone's cup with ginger ale.

"I propose a toast," he said.

Everyone lifted a glass.

"To the retirement of Pizzazz, the ultimate hamster," Roscoe continued.

"Wait a minute—" Calvin tried again.

"Pizzazz was loyal and intelligent"—Jenny began a little speech—"though his heart was not into magic. He's earned a rest."

"Yeah?" Calvin asked.

"He's been retired," said Jenny. "Blackstone is my new magic animal. She is very . . . focused."

Calvin glanced at Blackstone. Yeah, he guessed Blackstone was focused, if focused meant asleep.

"So, Calvin," Ms. Eva said, "Pizzazz's co-owners—Jenny and I—would like you to take care of Pizzazz."

"My mother won't let me have two pets," Jenny added. "And, well, I don't know why, but Pizzazz always seemed to like you better than me." Jenny fixed Calvin with a solemn stare. "Do you promise to take good care of him? Pizzazz might not have been the best magic animal, but he sure is a great hamster."

What's going on? Calvin thought. He looked from Jenny to Ms. Eva to Pizzazz, who was cramming seeds into his hamster cheeks.

"Calvin," said Ms. Eva gently. "Jenny and I want to *give* Pizzazz to you."

Calvin checked out his parents' reaction. He didn't want them to shake their heads and toss out that word "responsible." Re-e-e-e. *Spon*sible. Like a door creaking, then banging shut.

But Mom and Dad were sipping their ginger ale, smiling. . . .

All *right*! Calvin cheered in his mind. All *right*.

As Calvin reached for Pizzazz's cage, Ms. Eva spoke one sentence that made Calvin's hand stop in midair.

Ms. Eva said, "Calvin, Pizzazz can also live with you."

Calvin was so amazed, he couldn't even cheer in his mind. Pizzazz would live with *him*. The hamster would be the first thing he saw in the morning, the last thing he saw at night. Pizzazz would be his pet to pat, his friend to hold, his warm buddy in animal skin.

All *right*! he thought again.

But then he had another thought.

Without Pizzazz, Ms. Eva might feel lonely.

And Pizzazz might feel lonely after school when Calvin stayed with Ms. Eva.

"Ms. Eva," he said, "do you think you would like Pizzazz to visit you each day after school?"

Ms. Eva grinned her graceful grin. "Such a fine, magic-doing, mail-checking, nest-building hamster? Of course I'd like him to visit."

"Each day?" Calvin asked.

"Each day," said Ms. Eva.

Mary Quattlebaum received a B.A. from the College of William and Mary and an M.A. from Georgetown University. She is the author of *Jackson Jones and the Puddle of Thorns* and of numerous children's magazine stories and poems. She directs Arts Projects Renaissance, a creative and autobiography writing program for older adults, and lives in Washington, D.C., with her husband, Christopher David, who began learning magic when he was eight years old and can still bake a cake in his top hat. The hamster Pizzazz is based on several lively hamsters cared for by the author and her three sisters and three brothers when they were kids.

Robin Oz studied painting in England at the Slade School of Art, University of London. She has illustrated several children's books, including *Me and My Aunts, Devin's New Bed, The Fight, Peanut Butter, Too Much Ketchup, Toast for Mom, Down by the Bay,* and numerous workbooks. She lives in Connecticut with her husband, Frank, and their four children, Cody, Cooper, Woody, and Hadley. The Oz family shares its home with three dogs, two guinea pigs, one rabbit, ten hamsters, two birds, four baby chipmunks, and probably a horse by the time this book is published.